Praise

"Buckhanon's debut anger, hope, and frustration....A moving and uplifting story of love and hope in the face of adversity."
—*Publishers Weekly*

"A realistic love story that's set against an urban backdrop as gritty as its characters are memorable."
—*People*

"A sensitive portrayal of young lovers that moves beyond gritty urban fiction. The novel's inspiring story has a message of hope that's sure to connect with readers."
—*Essence*

"Packs a swift, head-clearing emotional punch...She knows whereof she speaks, and is, therefore, able to give voice to her young heroes in an authentic, exhilarating way."
—*Elle*

"*Upstate* is intimate, wrenching...a story about love, surviving love, and the forgiveness that only love brings."
—Achy Obejas, author of *Memory Mambo* and *Days of Awe*

"Heartbreaking and true...I'd read it again just for the power of the language."
—Dorothy Allison, National Book Award Finalist and national bestselling author of *Bastard Out of Carolina*

"Wild and beautiful."
—Sapphire, national bestselling author of *Push*

UPSTATE

ST. MARTIN'S GRIFFIN
NEW YORK

UPSTATE

■ ■ ■ ■ ■ ■

Kalisha Buckhanon

www.stmartins.com

Library of Congress Cataloging-in-Publication Data

Buckhanon, Kalisha, 1977–
    Upstate / Kalisha Buckhanon.
      p. cm.
    ISBN 0-312-33268-8 (hc)
    ISBN 0-312-33269-6 (pbk)
    EAN 978-0-312-33269-3
    1. African American prisoners—Fiction. 2. African American
women—Fiction. 3. Fathers—Death—Fiction. 4. New York (State)—
Fiction. 5. New York (N.Y.)—Fiction. 6. Young adults—Fiction. I. Title.

PS3602.U264U67 2005
813'.6—dc22

                                                    2004056651

First St. Martin's Griffin Edition: January 2006

10 9 8 7 6 5 4

DEDICATED TO
MY MOTHER AND FATHER,
ANOTHER GREAT
LOVE STORY

ACKNOWLEDGMENTS

This book would not have been possible without the faith, support, energy, and brilliance of three women: my agent, Tracy Sherrod, my editor, Monique Patterson, and my teacher, Sapphire, who believed in *Upstate* when it was just an idea. I would like to thank the Illinois Arts Council and the Gwendolyn Brooks Center for Black Literature and Creative Writing at Chicago State University for their generous rewarding of my work. And finally, Mr. Tony Clark, Aicha Balla, Abigail Thomas, Elizabeth Bewley, Rebecca Heller, and the St. Martin's team for their diligent, inspiring work and care for my story.

PART **ONE**

January 25, 1990
Dear Natasha,

Baby, the first thing I need to know from you is do you be-lieve I killed my father? I need to know if you believe what everybody saying about me because I need to know if you got my back. Right now I don't know who in my corner and who ain't. I looked in the mirror this morning and I didn't see nothing. That's how I feel, like I'm nothing. Like no-body see me or hear me or care about me or care what I got to say. Ma told me that some of my cuzos say they gonna kill me when I get out, say they gonna put a shank in my throat just like everybody say I did my daddy. They saying I better hope I got to do time cause when I get out it's a wrap. But see, they don't know me like you do. They don't know what I been through like you do. You was the only person who ever listened to me, you mostly, maybe Trevon and Black. Sometimes Ma. But mostly you. Remember all the shit we used to talk about late at night on the phone? About dropping out of school and going to Mexico or down South or somewhere like that? About us opening up some businesses and shit? About my music and me balling and you doing hair and shit? I know you remember. I do. I re-member every word you ever said to me.

You thinking about me? I hope so because I'm thinking

about you. I know you hadn't heard from me, but I'm in a large holding cell right now with a bunch of other cats, they trying to decide if I should be transported because I'm a juvenile. But they gonna move me soon, that's for sure. I'll let you know when they move me and where I'm at. I'm not even supposed to be writing this and mailing it to you cause I ain't got those privileges where I'm at. But two cats been looking out for me these past few days said, Tell us what you need son and we can hook you up; they've been here many times before. I told them, I need to write my girl. They know a guard who keep the communication flowing between the outside and in, so that's why you getting this letter. Baby girl I miss your fine ass so much I can't even think about how I'm gonna get out of this shit. I can't believe I'm here. Don't even know how I got here. I don't care. I'm thinking about the last time we saw each other. It seem like just yesterday me and you was bugging out in St. Nick Park, jumping over cars and shit. Member that white man watering his plants on his fire escape, and how he hollered bout calling the pigs and Black threw a bottle up at his ass and told him to get out of our hood? That shit was wild, that shit was funny. It was fun, the best time in my life. Then remember me and you went up them high steps that go to city college, and you let me suck your titties and rub you until you got all creamy and wet? I know you wanted to do something, if Black and Laneice wouldn't have been all up in the business, laughing and shit. Mad because they wasn't getting none. Remember what you said when we was walking back down and you was buttoning up your shirt and patting your baby hair down? Remember when you said you loved me?

    Write back soon,
    Antonio

■

January 27, 1990
Dear Antonio,

What happened? Did you kill him? Did you really do it? It's been on the news, in the papers, everything. Everybody at school and on the block keep asking me, keep wanting to know if I was there and if I seen it and if I helped you keep it a secret. I keep telling them naw, I didn't have nothing to do with that shit, but they don't believe me. Popos been over here three times asking me questions. They keep asking me was you on drugs and did you hit me and stuff like that. I told them no, but they kept on asking and they wouldn't leave and Mommy was getting upset. So, I didn't want to, but I told them you get high. I lied and said you didn't do it that much, just once in a while. They asked me if you did crack and I said "Hell no! Antonio wasn't no hype, he just smoked weed that's all." I think they believe me because they ain't been back since. You know I would never give you up, I would never tell about any of the shit you did. That's how much I love you. I got your back baby, cause I know you would do the same for me. I miss you so much I can't even breathe. I can't even get on the train or the bus no more cause I'm so used to taking it with you. I been walking everywhere now, but I don't mind. It give me some time to think, to clear my head, to figure out what the hell is happening with you, with me, with everything.

People at school won't stop staring at me and asking me questions. And Mr. Lombard, with his two-faced racist ass, had kept me in class after algebra wanting to know if I was okay and if I needed to talk to somebody. I didn't tell him shit either. I told him I was fine and I just wanted to go home so I could get ready to fix dinner cause Mommy was working late. I still ain't forgot about how he lied on me and said I was talking in class when I wasn't and I got in detention hall for a week. Don't try to be my friend now. But anyway, that's off the subject of what happened. I want you to tell me what happened. I promise to God swear on my daddy's grave that I won't tell nobody, not anybody, not even one living soul, not even Mommy. Just tell me. It won't make no difference. What I said that night was true.

Love Always,
Natasha

▪

February 1, 1990
Baby Girl,

This the deal yo, I can't talk about nuthin. I don't want to tell you what happened unless we face to face in private. I

*can't talk about nuthin. Everybody up in my business, out
to get me. I can feel it. I can tell. I can see everybody looking at me, I can hear them talking about me. Them motherfuckers opened your letter. They opened my shit and read
it. When I got the envelope, it was ripped in half and the
letter looked like it had been wet up. So, I know they reading this. I know they read everything I write. I wanted to
tell the cracker who brought it to me that he ain't had no
right to read my baby's shit, that it was between a man
and his woman and that's always sacred, but I didn't say
nothing. I just shook my head, cause I'm not trying to make
no trouble. I'm trying to get out of here. They not gonna get
me on some dumb shit. They not gonna win. So, to whoever
reading this, fuck you and your mama too. Fuck you over
and over and over again. I hope you die.*

*I been sent up to another facility right now.—It's on
some island right off the Bronx. Natasha, they put chains
around my ankles and connected me to a lot of other cats being transported from Manhattan in this big van. The ride
was bumpy, but quiet. Nobody said a word, nobody looked
at each other. When we got to the new joint, they unchained
us in this big room that looked like a warehouse and told
us to take off all our clothes. We had to stand there naked.
I was shaking it was so cold, and one by one they searched
our mouths and other places I don't want to tell you about.
I got my own room with a tiny cot, a toilet with a sink on
top, and this really long, narrow window that's about
three feet tall. The walls is white concrete like in the pj's.
I'm writing really fast cause I wanna finish this letter be-*

fore dark. There's no light, when the sun goes down, that's it. But I don't care. At least I'm not in a holding cell no more with twenty other funky cats and a stopped-up toilet like I was in Manhattan. People keep coming to talk to me—these court-appointed lawyers from someplace called the People's Advocacy or something like that. So far, it's been three different lawyers—this blond lady, some nerdy black dude, and now this fat white guy. Every time they switch they tell me the other one got busy cause they're overloaded with cases. I just say, Oh well as long as you know I'm not a murderer and what I did was in self-defense. I don't think any of them believed me though, cause they all said, That's what they all say and let me decide your defense. I feel a million miles from Harlem. But I think I can see the Empire State Building from here. I wish I could tell you everything that's happened to me, but it seem like it happened so fast I can't remember nothing.

A neighbor in my building called the popo's on the night everything went down. She had heard all the noise coming from my apartment, but when they came my mother answered and told them everything was alright. They came back a few days later after my daddy didn't show up for work for two days and we didn't answer the phone. My mother begged me not to open the door, begged me not to fess to anything, but I pushed her off me and told her that I was a man and I would live up to what I had done. I opened the door myself and took them to where my daddy was. They threw me down on the ground in front of Ma, Trevon, and Tyler. I put my hands behind my head—I didn't resist. But they didn't care.

They put their knees in my back and twisted my arms anyway when they put the handcuffs on. They took me to a police station all the way downtown and fingerprinted me and took a mug shot. They left me in a dark room with a slide-back window overnight. They didn't give me nothing to eat or drink. They didn't let me out to go to the bathroom and I had to whizz in the corner cause I was already a little sour under the arms, just from being scared and getting roughed up, and I didn't want to piss on myself and smell like that too. Next thing I knew, I was in this big room all by myself with three cops asking me why I stabbed my father over a dozen times. By then, I was having second thoughts about confessing so I just lied and said I didn't do nothing until they got tired of screaming and yelling at me. They just handcuffed my hands and ankles together, and put me in this long hallway where other guys kept getting called in one by one to this room that I really couldn't see into. I asked the dude sitting next to me what was going on, and he said something about rain. When they finally brought me in there, I realized it was a courtroom and I was standing before a judge. This blond lady I never seen before—that was the first lawyer—said something about entering a plea of guilty by reason of insanity and I yelled, No I'm not crazy! The judge stopped everything and told my lawyer to take me back and calm me down and get our story straight before we show our faces again in his courtroom. They took me back to the first room and I was waiting for the lawyer to show up so I could explain to her that I was just trying to stop my daddy from hitting my mother and it was an accident and

I'm not crazy I just stabbed him too hard when I just meant to scare him, but she never showed back up.

But Natasha I do want you to know I'm okay. I want you to know that you all I been thinking about and there ain't shit that's gonna tear us apart—not the cops, not these pen walls, not my daddy, nothing. I need you to come see me soon. I need to see your face so bad it hurts. I can't have no phone calls right now but we need to talk to each other in person so I can tell you what happened.

Write back soon,
Antonio

■

February 4, 1990
To My Baby:

Okay, so you still didn't go into details about what really happened, but it don't matter to me anyway. When I told you I loved you, I really did mean it. I'm glad I said it then because if I would have waited I would have never got to tell you face to face, just in a letter and that's not the right way to do it. So, I'm not gonna ask you no more what happened. I just know that whatever it was, it wasn't on you. It wasn't your fault. So, all that matter to me is that I know it wasn't your fault and you know I believe you didn't never want to hurt nobody. I walked past your locker today in the C wing. I know that ain't my wing and I wasn't supposed to be over there, but I think in my mind

I kind of hoped that you might be standing there waiting for me after lunch the way you used to. Of course you wasn't, but I was glad I walked by anyway. It kind of smelled like you when I walked by. Not no bad smell cause I can see your face right now all twisted up. Naw it was real good. That black licorice oil you wear and Cherry Now n' Laters you like and that coconut hair grease I used to put on your scalp before me or Laneice braid your hair. That's one of the things I love about you, the way you smell. Sweet all the time, like a girl. I bet you wanna know some of the other things I love about you. Well, I like the way you kiss me all deep, the bumpy curls on your head that are soft like cotton balls, the muscles in your arms and your stomach, the way you say my name, the way you put your palms on your cheek sometimes when you talk, that birthmark on your left shoulder, and the way you say other words like *son* and *for real* and *baby* sometimes (when we doing it). What you love about me? You never told me before so might as well tell me now.

Love,

Natasha

■

February 4, 1990
Dear Natasha,

They gonna let my mother come see me. I don't know the ex-act day yet, but my lawyer asked me if there was anything

I needed and I told him I wanted to see my family. He said
he could try to get me that privilege since I'm only sixteen
and all. So, they gonna let her come. You try to come too. I
really need to see you. I can't write much cause the sun is
already down and I can hardly see in the moonlight. Just
try to come see me.

    Love,
    A

■

February 7, 1990
Dear Antonio,

I talked to you mother and I think we all gonna come up
there and visit you this weekend, especially since your
birthday coming up. I had planned on buying you some
new kicks and a cap and maybe even a chain if I had
enough. Wish I could cop you a nickel bag. The lawyer
said family only, but Black said we could lie about it. He
said that when his cousin was moved upstate from
Riker's, the whole school came to see him and his
cousin's moms just kept on telling the guards, "My man
kept me real busy." I thought that shit was funny. So, we
gonna be there on Sunday. I think that only four or five
people can go. I know your mother said she going, and
she gonna bring Trevon because he 13 and old enough.
But she said she didn't want to bring Tyler. She said he
was too young, that she didn't want him to see his big

bro like that. I think he would love to see his big bro no matter what, but I guess that's her son so she gotta right to do what she want.

I know your problems are bigger than mine right now, but Antonio I just have to say I'm so sick of hearing my mommy's and stepdaddy's mouths I don't know what to do. All they talk about is this shit that happened and how they told me to stay away from you. I wish I could tell them to go to hell, but I can't. I wouldn't have nowhere else to go. I don't want to do like Drew did when Mommy got with Roy, move to Grandma's house in the Bronx. It's too far from school and my friends and you. I'm a Harlem Chick 4 Life!!!!!! That's why I'll be glad when all this shit is over and you get out because I think that we should get our own place. I think that we should just go and apply for one of those nice, new buildings that they fixing up finally around here, and we can stay in one of them. I went past one the other day, on 123rd and 8th. It's going to be called "Frederick Douglass Gardens" when it's finished. Wouldn't that be nice baby, to live in something called Frederick Douglass? At least I know that Frederick Douglass was black and he tried to free the slaves, I think. He was somebody who was brave and didn't take no shit and stood up for his rights. Right now, it's nothing but a big hole in the ground and a bunch of bricks and dust and wood and stuff. But they got a big billboard picture of what the building gonna look like and it's nice. It looked like a bunch of connected houses, with two and three stories. Not like the brownstones all stuck together or the pj's, but like real houses with a balcony and white paint and a nice little window on the front door. It was this nice Dominican man outside working on the building. He said he was the supervisor for the construction, so I figured he would know about moving in. So I asked him how you could move in. He told me they're condos and you had to buy them. I told him I wanted to try and he said that it was really hard because there was something like forty thousand applications for twenty houses. I told him I didn't think that there was even forty thousand people in Harlem, but I guess there are. Then he said that some of the applications was from people overseas and I wondered why somebody would want to move from overseas to Harlem, but I didn't ask him. I was running late for my hair appointment on 110 and Columbus. But he told me to call the phone number that was on the sign. That there was a lottery for people from the community, which I guess meant us. He was real nice. I gave the number to Mommy when I got home but she was too tired from work to call.

Well, how you doing? Tell me some more about what it's like in there. Is it a bunch of faggots running around, trying to feel your booty? Antonio, you better promise me that you don't do nothing like that. You better promise me you don't turn homo. You will go to hell if that's what you start doing. That's nasty and it's a sin. Matter of fact, any sex is a sin if it's not a man and wife who are married. That's why I think Antonio we shouldn't do it anymore. Antonio, I love the way you make me feel, like I'm a real woman and you make me wanna cry sometime it feel so good, but I feel really guilty that we did it and I'm not a virgin anymore. I didn't tell you because I didn't want you to snap, but Mommy tried to take me to the clinic on 116th and Lenox a couple weeks ago to get me that shot, but I wasn't about to do that shit. I wasn't about to get all fat and disgusting and have all my hair fall out. I told her we wasn't doing nothing. How could we? I told her, "You and Roy watch me like a hawk, y'all watch every move I make." If they knew I was skipping school and lying about track practice to be with you, they would kill me. So, I committed two sins: fucking and lying.

This Sunday in church with Grandma, when the preacher called people to the altar, I was the first in line. I think I want to get saved, to get baptized for real this time, not like when you a kid and you don't know what's going on. I don't know what happened to me. I just started crying and I couldn't stop. I was mostly thinking about how I was going to go to hell for having sex outside marriage, for lying to my mother. Then, I thought about how maybe that was God's punishment for you was to put you in jail because we sinned. And I just couldn't stop crying and shaking and then my legs got weak and I fell to the ground and I was crying and screaming and people started fanning me and putting their hands on me and the holy women started singing and the organ started going real fast and loud in my head, and I heard somebody scream "Save this child Jesus" before I passed out.

Love,

Natasha

■

February 11, 1990
Dear Baby Girl:

You looked so good this weekend I thought about just saying fuck it and trying to fight my way out of here. I thought that maybe if I just lay low and act all sweet and innocent that these co's will let their guard down around me, and I could pull a fast one on them like Jack Nicholson in One Flew Over the Cuckoo's Nest. *My mother used to make me watch that shit all the time when it came on late at night on cable, and I remember the first time I saw it I cried cause he didn't get away in the end. I bet I could get some of these older cats to help me out. They call me young blood cause I just made seventeen. It's two named Mookie and MGD who kinda look after me. I eat and lift with them and shit. They call me Bird because they say I got a bird chest, and I told them motherfuckers that's all right cause I'm gonna be eighteen and I'm gonna keep drinking my milk and grow up and whoop all they asses. But for real though, you looked real sweet and luscious in all that pink. I see you wore that little Karl Kani shirt I bought you. I got XS so it could fit just like that, all tight around your tatas. I wished nobody else was there so I could put em in my mouth for a minute, suck them like you like. And I like your new do, all braided tight and long down your back. That shit is hot. But the kiss was nice, it was enough to hold me over for a minute. It was so soft and sweet and wet. It felt like wet grass between my toes when we let the hydrants loose in the summer, or soap bubbles before you squeeze them too tight. I love your lips. I can't stop thinking about them and I still got that lip gloss flavor on em cause I won't wash it off—I think this time it was peach and not strawberry like you normally wear. I smelled it in my sleep so I dreamed about us. You coulda gave me a little bit more you know, but I understand if you was embarrassed, with my mother and cousin and brothers and shit all around. You gonna have to come by yourself one day, if they let you. If you dress up and put on some makeup you could look eighteen, you would just have to think of something to tell your mother and your stepdaddy.*

I'm gonna have to finish this letter up because my lawyer is going to be coming here any minute now, and he wanted me to write down a minute by minute account or some shit like that of the day before it happened. I'm saying "it" and not murder because I ain't no murderer and you know that so we don't have to go over it again. But I haven't done it yet. I don't know why, I guess I just don't wanna think about it right now. So if I don't finish it then he can just be mad at me. I don't care if he get mad at me because he ain't gonna do shit but huff and puff and fiddle with his glasses and swirl that one long hair he got on his head around his bald spot and grab his briefcase and run out and say something like, Antonio I'm here for you, I'm trying to help you. If you don't want my help then fine, or some other crackerjack talk. But before I go, I want to tell you Natasha that I love you with all my heart and a man don't say that often so when he does, he means it. And you don't have to worry about me turning into no gay faggot. I'm 100, no fuck that, 200 percent strong Black man. I do love you, that's why if I find out that you messin around behind my back, giving it up to somebody else while I'm in here, then you won't have to worry about me going to jail because I will just kill myself. I'm serious. I will find something to slit my throat or hang some sheets from the ceiling or make one of these big, swole niggaz in here so mad at me that they break my neck. To answer your question from the last letter, or I don't know if it was a question but I'll respond, what we do together is not a sin. It's a sin when two people get down and they don't love each other and they in it just for the thrill of the moment, for a little bit of pleasure. But see me and you is like a team, like Adam and Eve in the Bible, so how can that possibly be a sin if we love each other? You're right, lying is a sin and fucking is too. But we don't fuck, we make love.

    Love always,

    Antonio

PS. You know what? I'm sick and tired of McDonald's and bologna sandwiches. Remember how me and you used to cut Mr. Lombard class every six and seventh period so we could go to McDonald's and get a vanilla shake and large fry and Big Mac to share? Well, Mr. Lombard don't have to worry about me skipping his class for Ronald McDonald no damn more. You know they feeding us Mickey D type shit, right? Every day and morning and noon and night. Mickey D's. In the morning we have them sponge pancakes and nasty eggs, and at lunch we have shitburgers and at night we have shit-burgers again. Sometimes they'll substitute a bologna sand-wich. When I first got here, I had to do number 2 all the time cause of all the Mickey D's. I was embarrassed, but everybody told me not to worry about it cause they all did it too. But know this much, when I get out of here, I don't want to see the golden arches ever again in my life!

February 14, 1990
Dear Sweety Pie Honey Bunch Baby Love Strong Black
  Man Antonio,

Happy Valentine's Day and Happy Belated Birthday! *Bonjour. Comment ça va? Je suis très fatiguée* and sad and missing you a lot. Okay, I tried a little bit of French. If Madame Girard come over and snatch this note I'm writ-ing to you, she can't say it don't have nothing to do with class. But I said *bonjour,* which means hello or good day. Then I said how are you and I'm very tired and you know the rest. Thank you for my card and the teddy bear and everything. It was so sweet. When Black gave it to me this morning and told me that you told him exactly what to go out and buy, I started crying a little bit, I ain't gonna lie. I'm glad you liked the way I looked this weekend. Me and Laneice stayed up all night doing my hair and I wore that shirt you bought me on purpose. Antonio, you so nasty asking for a kiss in front of your mother. You right, I was a little shame at first, but I forgot about them real quick when I felt your tongue in my mouth. On the way back, you know Trevon and Black was making fun of me, making sucking noises and shit. But your mother just looked at me and then looked at them and then looked back at me and smiled that little smile she does when she know me and you ain't been to the movies like we said. And she was just like, "Ain't nothing wrong with a little bit of kissing, nothing wrong with a little bit of love." When you get out, I'm giving you all the love in the world. And you getting out of there soon baby! Did you hear on the news that this man in South Africa named Nelson Mandela got out of jail after 27 motherfucking years for some shit he didn't even do? Can you imagine being locked up for 27 years for something wasn't even your fault? Mr. Lombard made us sit in a circle and shit and get all cozy and talk about it, and here everybody go looking at me. Like I know about it just cause you in the joint. All I'm thinking is, it gotta be some hope for you Antonio if this man can hold on for 27 damn years and not break. You can stay strong for the few months it's gonna take to get you out of there. You know what the best part was? His wife was waiting for him when he got out, just like I'm gonna be waiting for you.

But I guess you wanna know why I'm tired? Same old shit, different night. Mommy and Roy got into it last night—again. The worst part is I think it's my fault. You remember when I told you about those new houses that they're building? Well, I thought my mother wasn't paying attention to me and wasn't listening, but I guess she was. She called the number last week and went down to this place in Midtown where they help people like us, you know without any money, get houses. Well, Roy found out about it the other night cause me and my mother was at the kitchen table trying to figure out the paperwork. She needed me to help her understand stuff like combined household income and assets and net worth and all that stuff we learned in econ. So anyway, we sitting at the kitchen table with our pencils sharpened and the calculators out and going, and this nigga come in the house smelling like weed and acting a fool. He is just so ugly to me Antonio, with them big red bubble eyes and those little nasty braids sticking up on his head like ant legs. Mommy keep trying to tell him he ain't never gonna grow no dreads because he's losing his hair, that he just gonna have one or two locks hanging on for dear life, but I guess he's like Jesse Jackson and trying to keep hope alive. Me and my mother was having so much fun too. She was laughing and she had pulled out some of her old tapes, stuff like Chaka Khan and Patti Labelle and Regina Belle. She was even trying to sing a little bit, and she had just promised that she would do my hair for over the weekend. My mother hasn't done my hair in so long Antonio, so I was getting excited just thinking about sitting between her legs while she parted my hair and rubbed my scalp until I got sleepy like a baby. But Roy messed all that up real quick, just like he been messing shit up for the past two years he been in our lives. He came in the kitchen and sat in the chair all backward. He said, "Denise what you doing?" and my mother just told his ass, "Nothing Roy, it don't concern you," which made me think that if we get this house he won't move in, which would be perfect. So he was like, "What you mean it don't concern me? Why you gotta be all bitchy? I just asked a question." So she lit a cigarette, which meant she was getting nervous cause Mommy only smoke when she nervous, and she told him, "I'm thinking about trying to buy me something." And Roy was like, "You need all them papers just to buy something? Must be a pretty big something." Then she said, "It is big. I want to buy a home." And he started laughing, howling really, all loud and sloppy and exaggerated. And I was thinking it really ain't that funny so he must be just trying to hurt Mommy. And I was right, cause he started going on and on about how nobody was gonna give her a house cause she didn't even have her high school diploma and couldn't pass the GED and she couldn't pay for a house and then she started saying that he wasn't no better and he couldn't help her do shit and she could do bad all by herself. Before I knew it, she had scooped all the papers up and stuffed them in the kitchen junk drawer. That was the end of that.

I just got up and went into my room and shut the door and turned up my Queen Latifah record real loud so I wouldn't have to hear all the arguing. I pulled out a picture of my daddy when he was alive and when I was first born, you know the one I showed you that looks kind of orange, with me and Mommy and Daddy and those fake trees in the back and I had those two Afro puffs and a sailor suit on? And I was mad at my daddy, mad at him because he had to leave me and my mother and die. Then I got mad at the world for the fire that took our building and my daddy. I mean Antonio why did MY father have to die? Out of all the daddies in the world, God just had to take mine. I was only eleven. Eleven years ain't no time with your father. It's not fair. It's not right. And I got mad at you too, Antonio. Mad because you couldn't talk to me about what was happening in your house and what was going on so I could have tried to help you, so you wouldn't leave me too. Sometimes, I wonder what the point of loving somebody is, if all they gonna do is turn around and leave you in the end. I hope you got a good lawyer, because I can't stand the thought of you being locked up for life. Because in that case, you might as well be dead to me. I'm not trying to make you feel bad, but I just don't know how much more I can take. I'm real lonely out here in this world, on the outside like you like to call it.

Au revoir (that means until I see you again and I will see you again soon),

Natasha

PS. *J'adore* Antonio!!!!!!!!!!!!

■

February 18, 1990
Dear Natasha,

Okay there is not much I can say in this letter. I'm gonna have to wait until I see you again because like I told you, these crackers read my shit and I don't want to say anything that might incriminate me. My lawyer told me not to talk to anybody about anything, because it could all be evidence against me in the end. But baby, please don't be mad at me right now. I can't take you being mad at me right now. That thought is like a dagger in my heart, or swallowing a razor and shitting it out. Remember when we were at the library and you found that book showing how white folks threw slaves in the ocean with anchors and chains around their ankles, so they could sink and never come up again? That's what you made me feel like, a slave in the middle of the ocean with a anchor around my feet. Like I was in some deep dark ocean where nobody loved me or cared about me, like I was in the dark with water all around me and inside of me. Like I should just give up and not even try to fight or struggle anymore. When I read your letter my stomach got all twisted and I got a taste in my mouth like the cod liver oil my mother used to force down my throat when I was sick. You all I got right now, you and my mother and that's it. Maybe Trevon and Black, but it's a different type of loyalty we have. I ain't a punk, but the only thing I can say right now is that I need you, Natasha. I never thought I'd say I need no female, but I need you right now and I can't stand the thought of you being mad at me. I can't tell you totally what happened the night Daddy died, and I wish I could because I know that it would help you believe in me. Let's just say it's not what you or other people think.

All I can say is that my lawyer is a good guy and I think he really working hard for me. He joke with me all the time about how I'm going to be back in school and back on the courts in no time. He told me that all we have to do is get my story straight and argue that I snapped from seeing my father hit my mother one too many times and I couldn't take it anymore and that's why I did what I did. And that's the truth, it's not a lie. You'll hear in court what happened, the truth will come out when I have my day in court. They want to try me as an adult because I'm seventeen now. He told me that he's trying to persuade the judge that I shouldn't be tried as an adult, and he said that he is sure he can do that for me. Which means, Natasha, that the longest I can be locked up is until I'm 21 and that's not a long time for us to be apart. When I'm 21, you'll just be 20. When I get out we can get married real quick

and start a family and buy a house where you can do hair
or make clothes in the basement and I can have a music
studio or sumthin down there too. We can do it. We can get
through it and this can happen for us. I just need for you
not to be mad at me and not to leave me, just to stick by me
and not to leave me. Write me back as soon as you get this.

Love always and forever,
Michael Antonio Lawrence II

■

February 28, 1990

Antonio, I'm so sorry that it has taken me so long to answer your letter. I know you wanted me to write back as
soon as I got it, but the truth is, Roy had your letter and
was keeping it from me. Yeah, he read your shit. I saw an
envelope with New York State Inmate Correspondence Services balled up on the dresser in my mother's
room when she sent me in there to get her purse so I
could go to the corner store. And I snatched it off the
dresser and came out demanding to know who opened
my shit and who read it. And my mother looked like she
didn't know what I was talking about, and then Roy
started laughing that ole stupid laugh of his. Talking
bout, "Girl calm down. I just wanted to know what the
little nigger was talking about. You better write him
back soon, cause I don't want the young'un drowning in
the ocean." I don't know what happened, I just couldn't

take it anymore. I had to do something. I had to hit somebody. I hate him Antonio. I hate him so much. I just started screaming and kicking, and my arms were swinging around like the fan blades and I was saying, "I hate you I hate you I hate you!" over and over again. He was laughing at me the whole time, grabbing my arm and lifting me up off of my feet like I was a rag doll. And my mother was screaming, "Don't hurt her Roy! Don't hurt her please don't hurt my baby!" and then he finally put me down. I just left the house in a daze. I don't know how, but I ended up on the 2 going to the Bronx. I stayed at my grandmother's house this weekend. I'm not leaving. I'm not going back there. Drew was smart getting the hell out of that house when Roy came. I don't care what my grandmother say about trying to get along. I'm not going back.

So Antonio, I'm sorry that I didn't write back soon. I didn't get your letter and I thought you weren't thinking about me because you were too busy getting ready for your trial and stuff. Write me back soon. Or try to call me collect at my grandmother's house cause this is where I'll be for the rest of my life.

Love,
Natasha

■

March 1, 1990
Dear Whore:

Natasha you are a stupid bitch. You don't care about me.
All you know how to do is think about yourself. You don't
think about me waiting for your letter every day you don't
think about me calling your house and you're not there and
I don't know where you are if you dead or alive or if you
got somebody else. You're selfish and you get on my nerves
bitch bitch bitch hoe hoe hoe bitch I hate you
    With hate,
    Antonio

■

March 14, 1990
Dear Antonio,

I don't know what's going on with us. I don't know why
you're treating me like this but you need to chill. Stop
breakin' on me for something that wasn't my fault. Antonio, I miss you so much my stomach been hurting and
I can't eat no more. I was even throwing up the other
night and Roy black ass gonna tell Mommy, "You better
go get the girl a piss test and see if she pregnant." I told
him, "Leave me the fuck alone," and called him a gorilla-
looking son of a bitch under my breath. Why he always
on my case? But I miss you so much Antonio, I'm gonna

die. I swear I'm gonna just lay down and not get back up.
I think I lost about ten pounds, maybe even more. Them
tight skirts you used to like on me ain't even tight no
more. I don't have a belt tight enough to keep em up.
Antonio, I'm so worried about you I don't know what to
do. I NEEEEEEDDDDDD to see you. I don't know
why you not calling me. What did I do to you? I can't
even eat and I can barely sleep because I'm so worried
about you and scared that you hate me. I had to leave Mr.
Lombard class the other day because I was crying again.
He tried to talk to me after class again, telling me that
he was always there to talk and asking me if I needed
counseling or some shit like that. I don't know why that
white man always trying to be my friend after class when
he treat me like shit in class, but whatever. I don't know
if you got beat up in there or what. I talked to your mom
and she said that you were calling the house. I asked her
if you had asked about me and she said that you said you
were through with me. She asked me, "What did you do
to my son?" and I told her I didn't do nothing. I explained to her about why I didn't write you back, about
Roy and stuff, and she just nodded her head and said
something like, "Antonio just acting real sensitive right
now." I don't think she believe me because she been acting funny now when I stop by, so I don't stay long no
more. Or maybe she just sad, real sad that you ain't there
and Mr. Lawrence is dead and Tyler and Trevon is asking
her why they daddy gone and they big brother is locked
up. So I didn't ask if I could go with them to see you this

weekend. If your mother's mad at me and you're mad at me, then I didn't want to place myself in a uncomfortable situation.

But I just want you to know that I do love you. I'm sorry if I wasn't thinking about you and what you're going through. I guess I shoulda wrote to you even if you didn't write me, and I promise it won't happen again. I promise you I won't ever hurt you again or ever cheat on you in life. The prom is coming up and I swear to you I'm not going with anybody. Me and Laneice and some of my cousins might all go together and wear the same colors, but that's it. You'll be there in my heart. I'll put your picture in my purse. Write me back soon or call me when you get a chance. I'm back at home now with my mother, so you can call me there. I will sit at home all week if I have to and wait for your call.

Love,
Natasha

■

March 17, 1990
Dear Natasha,

Baby, I'm so sorry for everything I ever did to you. I'm so sorry for making you upset and making you cry and I promise I will never do it again. When I heard your voice on the phone the other day I just felt so stupid and mad at myself for treating you the way that I treated you and saying the things that I said and returning your letters. You better keep your promise and send them back because I want to read each and every one of them and write you back for each and every one. I was so relieved when you picked up the phone and took my call. I thought that you would hate me after the way I treated you and how I acted. MGD and Mookie was laughing at me when I was talking on the phone with your ass, calling me whipped and sprung and shit cause I was apologizing so much. They was like, Youngblood got it bad, youngblood got the jones. But I didn't care. I love you. You're my woman, my lady, my girl, my heart. Nothing else mattered when I was talking to you. My trial is about to start soon, and it's gonna be over quick because everybody gonna see the truth about what happened. And when they see the truth and see I ain't no monster and that I'm a real person with feelings who wouldn't kill his daddy for nothing, they gonna let me go and then we can be together forever. We can be with each other forever. I want to marry you. Natasha, will you marry me?

Sincerely,
Antonio

■

March 21, 1990
Dear Antonio,

Yes!!!!!!!!!!!!!!!!!!!!
Love, Natasha

■

March 26, 1990
Dear Natasha,

Nubian Princess
Always got my back
Totally real and fresh
Antonio's woman for life
Smile like sunshine
Hair like silk
All the Woman I need
   Love you forever,
   Antonio

■

March 30, 1990
Dear Antonio,

Your mother is real excited about us getting married. She told me that I should make you buy me a big diamond ring when you get out—in a few weeks, she said. You didn't tell me baby you was getting out in a few weeks, did you? Anyway anyway, it's this place up on 125th and 7th where I know we could get a big diamond real cheap. It might be stolen from somewhere, but it'll still be cheap. I'm sure if you got about a hundred or two dollars we could get one. After the rings we can get a car, then an apartment to call our own, and then a house. Remember when Black had stole that Malibu on 145th, by the library, and we drove up and down FDR all night? You looked so fine behind the steering wheel. I was shocked that you could drive. You never told me you were that good behind the wheel. Then you promised me you would teach me.

When I was smaller and my feet couldn't even reach the pedals, my daddy used to let me sit on his lap and take hold of the wheel while he put his hard hands on top of mine. One time I drove almost all the way down 125th when it was Christmastime. I counted all the lighted Christmas trees hanging above the streetlights. That was one of the only ways I even knew it was the holidays. I counted seven Christmas trees in the sky before my daddy bounced me off his knee real fast. He had spotted this cop pulling up behind us when we passed 5th and he was worried about getting pulled over cause his license was suspended. Daddy slowed down, turned off the radio, and I swore I could hear his heart beating as loud as mine the whole way, and I kept looking back to see if a police car would be behind us with its lights flashing and then the cop would pull us over and throw my daddy on the car and handcuff him while his head was down low and I would have to walk to my uncle's house around the corner on 124th and Lenox and maybe just maybe somebody I went to school with would see me walking and ask me why or see my daddy in the police car and ask me why and I would have to tell them and be laughed at the next day at school. We was quiet the whole way home until we made it to our building, where my mother was looking out of the window on the fourth floor, waiting for us with Drew in her arms because he was still just a baby. She couldn't start dinner until Daddy came home with the groceries, and I remember how happy my daddy looked bringing the groceries up the stairs, staring at my mother like he couldn't wait to make another baby with her. We were a regular happy family back then, before the fire, before Roy, before Drew left to live with Grandma. Me and you gonna have a family like that one day, we gonna start all over again and get it right.

With love,

Natasha

April 5, 1990
Natasha,

Baby, I'm scared. I don't think I want you to come to the trial. My lawyer said that he might call you to testify, to talk about my character and to talk about my relationship with my mother and father. But he said that most likely he won't need you, since you can't—what was the word—substantiate any abuse or anything. He asked me if you knew about it and I told him you didn't know shit about it because I wasn't trying to expose you to anything. Tyler and Trevon definitely gonna have to talk, maybe Black since he

*my best friend and he was in our house a lot. I don't think
I want anybody I know to come to the trial. It's a lot of
things you don't know about me, things that have happened
to me in my life that I'm embarrassed to have people know.
My lawyer been practicing with me, he been schooling me
on what to say and how to act and how to look at the jury
and the judge and all that so they can be sympathetic for
me. He told me that it was only about five of us on the jury,
you know, black people. He said that he tried to get more,
but he couldn't. He said that he tried not to pick no old people or no Christians because they was the worst when it
came to feeling sorry for somebody, especially me since people
think that the worst thing in the world is killing one of
your parents. He said if it was my mother, I could have
hung it up, but since it was my daddy—a man—that I
have a big chance. He said that I have a real chance. I really ain't never talked about God a lot or went to church,
mostly cause my family didn't, but I guess you should pray
for me. I think that's gonna help.*

    Love,
    Antonio

▪

April 8, 1990
Dear Antonio,

How can you ask me not to come to your trial? Baby you
KNOW I gotta be there for my man! How you gonna

ask me to not come down there so I can see you every day? I'm gonna get on the train and come to the courthouse every day. Fuck school, cause I ain't learning shit in that dump anyway. Everybody been looking at me at lunch, in the halls, in the courtyard, talking bout "Ah-hah, yo man locked up." Like you was a nobody or something. These the same motherfuckers used to laugh in your face, used to be your friends. And to think, we actually worry about who like us and who don't, when even the people who act like they like you ain't got your back when you need it. Plus Mommy don't care if I go. All she can think about is Roy, so she won't know no better. I told you that your lawyer and the popos and everybody else been trying to get me to talk, but I told em I don't know shit. But if they want me to say something good, I'll be there. I wouldn't miss that for the world. I'm gonna look real good for you too, baby. Every day I'm gonna have a new outfit, something fierce and sexy, so you can have something to think about at night when you can't sleep cause you thinking about being with me. And don't worry about me hearing anything at the trial that's gonna make me stop loving you. THAT is never going to happen. I ain't never gonna stop loving you as long as I live. So, make sure that you look for my face out in the audience, whenever you thinking about giving up or thinking the judge don't like you, know that you got somebody out there who love you and got your back.

Love, your wife,

Natasha

April 12, 1990
Hey boo,

Never thought the infamous Antonio Michael Lawrence would be saying this, but God I miss school!!! I miss that punk ass principal Mr. Diggs, I miss them damn security guards chasing my ass around and making me go to class, I even miss those nasty slices of pizza at lunch. Yo those things taste like rubber, but I don't think anything could be worse than McDonald's all the damn time. I miss wilding out in the hallway and joshing with Black in class, casing on people and shit. Talking about each other's moms and each other's dicks. I even miss my teachers, a little bit at least. I miss driving them up the wall. Madame Girard still crazy, still running around with them bright ass colors on talking about she celebrating Mardi Gras? Yo that bitch was crazy. I know she used to be cussing me out in French and knew I hadn't studied that shit so I wouldn't be able to tell. You said Mr. Lombard getting on your nerves? What's new? Mr. Cook still bringing in his whack ass rhymes, trying to get us to listen to that shit? He need to stick to teaching English and leave hip-hop to the pros. But I guess I really liked Mr. Cook cause he came to work looking nice every day in his suits and shit, although I don't know why he was dressing up just for us. But he used to tell me all the time, Antonio, you gotta dress for success. That's what he always used to say when I rode him about them tight pants and his shoes shining like new money. I mean, his wife is mad fine, so I don't know why she didn't dress him better. He used to say with that funny ass voice, Black man got hard enough boat to row in this country without being harshly judged for their appearance. You need to pull your pants up and tuck your shirt in young man. Or he used to call me son sometimes, and I imagined he was my daddy. Member all that "Crackdown on Putdowns" shit he tried when he got sick of us making fun of him for that Jamaican accent? That week, I musta got put out about forty or fifty times cause I couldn't stop making fun of that motherfucker when he was up there trying to teach us that Catcher in the Rye *shit. Now that I'm locked up, I kind of wish I woulda listened to him a lot more.*

I didn't want to tell nobody, but I really did like that book, The Catcher in the Rye. *Yeah yeah yeah, I know I told you I didn't read it and I made you write that damn narrative essay or whatever the hell it was for me. But I did read it, matter of fact I read it twice. I was really feeling all that Man vs. Society and Man vs. Self shit that Mr. Cook was telling us Holden was going through. Like I was really identifying with the part when he fell down the steps and slipped on them peanuts or cashews or whatever the hell it was, cause I thought that meant that it was easy for you to kind of walk into stuff in life that could make you fall, that could trip you up just when you thought you couldn't get any lower. That's what I used to think before this shit, but now I'm like Holden Caulfield slipping on peanuts. Shit only got worse for me. I'm gonna tell you a little secret that you can't tell nobody and you better not show nobody this letter cause then they'll know. But remember that part in the very end of the book, when Holden sister, I think her name was Phoebe, was on that carousel and he couldn't stop looking at her and he started crying because he thought she looked so pretty? And then it started to rain, and he couldn't even move because he was just so happy looking at her? I had started crying on that part, cause I was thinking about this one time that my mother had took me and Trevon all the way to Coney Island to walk on the boardwalk and ride the Ferris wheel. I had stood down at the bottom cause you could only ride two at a time and Trevon wouldn't ride with nobody but Ma. But she looked pretty like that, with her bright red lipstick on and them big doorknocker earrings and her baseball cap. She looked like mad young and I had looked at her in a different way that day, like I could see why my daddy fell in love with her. I had wanted to write about that for my narrative essay or response or whatever that shit was called, but I guess I didn't want to worry about the fellas laughing at me.*

Yeah, I miss that place, never thought I'd say that shit but it's true. Most of all, I miss looking at your fine ass every day, passing notes and shit, sneaking feels in the stairway. I can't wait to get back. I'm gonna be a different person. I mean that Natasha. If I get out of this shit, Michael Antonio Lawrence II is gonna be a new man. I made a promise to God that if he let me out then I'm gonna be the person that him and my mother would want me to be.

I promise I'm gonna do all my homework, I'm not gonna make the subs cry, I ain't gonna crack on nobody in class, I ain't gonna cheat off my boys work. Matter of fact, I'm gonna make them start studying. Imagine that, me and Black and some of our other cats in the library or at the crib with a book open and the TV off. I can't wait to see that one. But I'm gonna do it. I'm gonna make it happen. I'm gonna change, cause if me and you gonna do this man and wife shit, then I gotta get my shit together. That's on the real. I gotta go to college, get a good job, make sumthin out of myself so I can do right by you and the kids. I ain't gonna fuck up like my daddy did. I ain't gonna have my kids living in no projects, wearing hand-me-down shit and lying to folks over the phone cause I can't pay my bills. I ain't gonna drink myself silly and beat my wife and my kids cause I ain't a man and I can't pay my bills. I ain't gonna fuck no young tricks in my wife bed cause I don't have respect for her. I ain't gonna do none of that. I'm gonna be a good man.

    Love, your husband,
    Antonio

■

April 19, 1990
Dear Antonio,

You looked so good today in the courtroom. I ain't never seen you in a suit before and you sure looked fresh in it.

It made me think that maybe if we went to church like my grandmother always trying to get me to do, I would have seen you in a suit before. And maybe if we went to church, God would smile down on us more like my grandmother say and this wouldn't have happened. But, oh well, it did happen so here we are. Anyway, I helped your mother pick out that suit. We went all the way to Macy's to get it. It cost almost 150 dollars, Antonio. Your mother said she had used some of the money she got from people after the funeral to buy it. She had wanted to buy you some of them corny ass loafers to wear with your suit, but I told her Antonio IS NOT gonna wear them shoes. She tried to challenge me, and said, "Little girl, I think I know my son better than you do." So I had to break her heart and let her know she didn't. I told her about them no-name jeans she used to get you from Conway, remember the ones with the pockets all high to your stomach and them thick cuffs at the bottom? I told her you used to take them jeans off in gym and wear sweats hanging down all day. She looked hurt about it, but at least she took my advice and we got the black sneaks. Who braiding your hair up in the joint? It looked all nice and neat and fresh. Let me find out you got a "girl"friend up in there! I'm just kidding. I know you wouldn't never leave me and go that way. I was surprised that things was so short today. I thought we was gonna be there a long time. I thought it was gonna be a lot more screaming and yelling and the judge banging his gavel and stuff like that. But everything was pretty chill, which was cool. The less action the better in this case, right? I think your lawyer real good. He did a good job talking to the jury about you, he made you sound real good. Not that you ain't real good anyway, but it seemed like you was going through some shit you wasn't letting me in on. I didn't know you was going through it baby. Why didn't you tell me? If we gonna be husband and wife, I'm gonna need to know these things. I'm gonna need to know about what's going on with you at all times, so no shit like this don't ever happen again.

Love,

Natasha

PS. Madame Girard want me to apply for this special program they got for kids who go to public school in New York City to go to France over the summer. She said that you could spend like a whole month in Paris over the summer, living with a family and taking classes and going to all these art museums and stuff. She told me she would write me a recommendation because I do good in her class. See Antonio, when you come back to school you gotta make sure you do good in her class so she can write you a recommendation and you can go too. Maybe we can get married before we go and this can be our free honeymoon. Think about it, okay boo?

Love again,

Natasha

April 23, 1990
Dear Natasha,

Baby, you don't know how good it felt to see you today. Did you notice anything different about me? I been lifting—I got muscles now. Three months in here and I ain't no bird chest no more. MGD and Mookie was riding me the other day at lunch, talking bout You done graduated, son—pre-K to kindergarten. When I get out and we finally get some time alone, I'm gonna put it down like I never did before. Baby, you gonna love my new body. I'm hard as a brick. I think that tomorrow if you sit right behind me we could be close enough to hold hands under the railing, behind my chair. I don't think the cops will notice if we be real low-key about it. I think that things is going real good for me with this thing. It seem like all the witnesses they have are doing a good job of really convincing the judge that I'm not a bad kid. I think I can feel real good about my lawyer. He's a cool dude, he's on my side. I guess I had watched too many movies where the court-appointed attorney wasn't shit, but he different with his nerdy ass. He always make sure that I get something real good to eat when I'm not behind bars, cause he know what I'm going through in there. The other day, he brought me some funny-smelling tie food or something like that, some of that Chinese shit. It was good though, a bunch of noodles in some peanut sauce. I never knew you could make sauce with peanuts, but I'm learning a lot of shit I never knew these days.

We got some psychiatrist test back today that they had did on me, and he said some corny shit like, By George Antonio you're a genius. And I told him to quit messing with me and he was like, No, according to these tests, you're in the mid to upper echelon or some shit of human intelligence. I was like get the fuck out of here, and he said he was serious. Then I told him, That's good shit. And he was like, Actually it isn't. He said he wasn't trying to get me down, but his job would be a lot easier if I was retarded. I thought that was some funny shit and we laughed, but I would rather go to jail than for people to think I'm a retard. Now, I never thought of myself as no genius. I wonder what my homeboys would think about that. I know none of my teachers would say that shit. I didn't do homework, ain't never made the honor roll in my life. I guess when I get out of here and change my ways, I'm gonna get on that motherfucker for real. Maybe I should forget about music and balling, and think about being a scientist or some shit like that. But back to the trial, I liked that one dude who got up and testified for me, the coroner or whoever who said that the angles of the entry wounds showed that my daddy was probably coming at me when I stabbed him. That bitch prosecutor tried to stare him down and shake him and keep asking him the same questions over and over again but in different ways. Did you catch that baby? I did. Well, he didn't shake. He stuck to what he said, which was that my daddy had to be coming at me. He wouldn't break for her. And I couldn't believe that Mr. Cook came through, that he showed up for me. With one of them tight suits on again. I

*think that was a big thing for us, cause my lawyer had
said when we were eating that tie shit, This was a good
day Antonio, a real good day. I think it was too. He told
me that between the experts and the character witnesses, I
would be straight.*

*But my family is coming up—my mother and my
brother and my partners are getting ready to get up there
and start talking about things I don't want to talk about,
things I don't want nobody to hear. I gotta get up there
too, and every day me and my lawyer be practicing what
I'm gonna say. He be cursing me out and shouting and getting real mean, but he just doing what he gotta do so I can
be prepared for anything that could come up. I think that's
the day I don't want you to come, when my family start
talking. I don't think I can take you hearing the truth
about me.*

*Sincerely,
Antonio*

■

April 27, 1990
My dearest Antonio,

It's late at night and I'm sitting out here by myself on
the fire escape, looking at 7th Ave, thinking about you
and how we used to sit out here and hug and laugh and
tickle each other and kiss real hard and long. I miss you
so much my whole body hurts. Mommy just went back

inside. I can still smell her Avon perfume, it's stuck in the air all around me, like she's still out here with me and holding me tight. Drew spent the night tonight. He said Grandma been acting a little cuckoo lately, making him clean greens and chitlins and turn soil and shit and he can't take it. Mommy tried to tell him that no matter where he went it was gonna be something he didn't like, and that he couldn't run away every time he didn't want to follow rules. So she told him since he made the choice to up and leave and help Grandma and live with her for a while, that he could only stay for the night and then he was gonna have to take his butt back to the Bronx. Roy wasn't even around, so I don't think she was trying to please him when she said it. I think she was really right and trying to teach Drew a lesson. I guess she was right. You can't have it your way all the time.

But he was sleep on the couch snoring and slobbing all over the pillows, and my mother had came out to put a blanket on him cause it's still a little chilly even though it's spring. So after she put the blanket on him, she came out to the fire escape to smoke a cigarette. She asked me if the smoke was bothering me, and I told her no. Then she asked me if I had smoked before, and I couldn't even lie. Hell, me and Laneice was smoking L's last night. I don't know what it is, but I always find it hard to lie to my mother. That shit is, like, almost impossible. I just started laughing and kind of whispered, "Yeah . . ." She didn't get mad though, she just told me that she wished she had never started and then told me I should stop while I still got a chance. She asked me how I was doing, and I told her I was okay. I started to tell her that I had been skipping school to come to your trial, but I figured I didn't want to hit her with too much at one time. The smoking was enough for one night. The school can't call cause our phone disconnected anyway. But she saw my notebook out and me writing, and she said, "Girl, you and them letters." I thought she was gonna say something smart or crack on me or whatever, but she didn't. She just kind of looked up at the sky, then down at the street cause it was so quiet and empty. I mean, there wasn't one car or one person on the block for a few minutes, and you know that never happens around here. Then she just kind of patted my shoulder and told me not to stay up too late. And here I am, staying up late writing to you. But Antonio, I'm going to have to wrap this letter up soon. I gotta do my science and English homework, plus I think I'm gonna go ahead and apply for that thing that Madame Girard want me to apply to. I think that it would be a good learning experience for me, like she said. I never really been out of New York. I been to Albany and Philly to visit some of my relatives, and I been down to VA and North Carolina. But shit, that's it. Imagine going all the way over the ocean. It's like 100,000 miles and it takes about eight hours on the plane. I never even been on a plane before. I think it would be amazing to look down and see the tops of all the buildings in Harlem, then New York, then the United States, and then all of a sudden the whole world.

Laneice flew one time, to Disney World with her church, and she told me that it looks like the sky done reversed itself. Like, it switched places with the ground. She said that's what people mean when they say they're walking on air, because when you look out the window and see the clouds below you, you feel like nothing can touch you. That's how I want to feel right now, like nothing in the world can touch me. (Except you.)

Love,
Baby Girl

■

April 30, 1990
Baby Girl,

I never thought I would ever see my mother as sad as I saw her today. I never ever seen my moms cry before, never, not even when Daddy was kicking her ass or when it wasn't no food in the house or when I fucked up in school. I bet she ain't even cry at the funeral, did she? You don't have to tell me, I know she didn't. I never knew before today how much my mother really loves me. I asked her a thousand times since that day, Ma, you still love me? Ma, you mad at me? And she always say that she would never stop loving me cause I was her firstborn and I came out of her body first and showed her what it meant to really be a woman, so she said that she would never stop loving me. But she ain't never answer if she was mad at me, she never answered that question straight. She just say stuff like, I'm sorry for what I put you through, or I should have left, or I wish things would have been better. So I guess she is kind of mad at me, at least a little bit. But after today, I know she still love me. I guess I didn't want you to know about the things that went on in my house, about that shit that go on behind closed doors that nobody wanna talk about. And I guess I didn't want you to be mad at me about letting shit go on. I should have been a man. I should have handled shit better.

I could handle it when Black got up there, told them about that night, how we came home and my mother was all beat up and I grabbed a knife out of the sink and me and my daddy got into it and I just tried to get him off my mother but I stabbed him instead, by accident. Maybe. I don't care if somebody reading this letter because I need to stand up and be a man and admit the truth to myself. I know Trevon was lying for me up there. I think he don't think it was a accident, and looking back I don't think it was either. I think I meant to do it. I meant to kill my father, Natasha. It wasn't an accident. I did it. I guess I'm just gonna have to live with that. I wanted to shut my ears and crawl down on the floor and die when Trevon started talking about how my daddy swelled up, how he got heavy, how him and me and my mother pulled him in the bathroom and left him there while me and my mom was trying to figure out what to do. Trevon helped me remember it, helped me remember how I felt, how my head was swimming and how I couldn't breathe or think or eat or dream about nothing but the body the body the body coming to get me and swallow me whole. I wanted to get up and go out of the room and cry by myself, like a man, but I know I couldn't get up and go nowhere. I know they would have wrestled me down on the ground and put their knees in my back and on my neck and made my mother cry even more, so fuck it, I just sat there and let tears come down my face. I tried to stop myself, but I just couldn't help saying, "I'm sorry Ma." I know I upset the court-room, but I couldn't help myself. Ma was really trying to get those people to believe her, to believe that I was a good son. But I know I wasn't. I lied, I got in trouble in school, I stayed out all night and had her worrying and shit. I guess I did all that shit cause I didn't want to be at home. I didn't want to see my daddy hitting her or drinking or running around with other women. I couldn't stand seeing Tyler and Trevon cry all the time. I couldn't stand that shit. I didn't want to see it. But if I would have known my mother was hurting and upset, I would have done bet-ter I really would have. I would have been a better son. I got a whole weekend to think about what I'm gonna say when I get up there, how I'm gonna get these people to be-lieve I'm not a monster.

With love,

A

May 1, 1990

Antonio, we can't change the past. We can only focus on the future. That's what Madame Girard and Mr. Cook and Mr. Lombard and my mother and my grandma always say to me when I'm mad about something or feeling like I need to fight. Like when the fire happened and we lost my daddy and all our stuff and we had to go live in that shelter while we waited for an apartment to open up. I was so mad at everybody and all I could think about was killing somebody or setting something on blaze so I could burn up too and go be with my daddy again. That's why we got put out of the shelter, cause they had found me in the bathroom setting towels on fire. Cause I wanted to burn myself. I really did. I wanted to commit suicide, if you can believe that about me. I never told you I did something like that, but it's amazing what you can tell somebody in a letter that you can't tell them face to face. But my mother wasn't even mad at me because she said that was just my way of expressing myself, and that I would have to find a new way of dealing with things. She said that Daddy wasn't coming back and we needed to think about the future now, what we were going to do with the hand God dealt us. That's what I'm telling you and that's what you need to believe.

Antonio, I don't love you any different than I did before you got locked up. And no, I don't think you crazy and I would never think you crazy. You had to do what you had to do, right? You didn't mean to do it, and I know that if you could change the past you would. You would have done something different. I know you would have. I have no doubt in my mind that you would have made a better choice. So stop calling yourself a monster, okay? You starting to make me worry about you. If you think that's what you are, then that's how it's gonna sound when you get up there to tell your side of the story. And that's not how you want it to come out. So, you just gotta stay strong and believe in yourself, so you can get up there and do what you gotta do, so you can get out of this situation and we can be together. Just think about that and let that help you whenever you start thinking about what a bad person you are. Stay strong for me, so we can get past this and move on with our lives and go on to do all those things we talked about, okay?

Head up,
Natasha

■

May 1, 1990

Well baby, my lawyer said I did okay, but I know he just trying to make me feel good. I know I blew it today. I didn't mean to get mad, but I just couldn't help it. All that shit that bitch was saying to me, bringing up shit that didn't have nothing to do with what happened that day. I mean, what the fuck do the fact that I got suspended this year for fighting got to do with what happened on that day between me and my daddy? That ain't got shit to do with nothing, but when my lawyer object she wanna say some shit about establishing my aggressive personality and propensity for rage and all that other shit. Using all them big words to get it twisted for everybody. Then she gonna have the nerve to ask me why I didn't call the pigs or why I didn't tell nobody at school or a counselor or my doctor or whoever about what was going on in my crib. What is that bitch thinking? Oh yeah, while doc sticking a big needle in my butt I'm just gonna be like, "Yeah, Daddy beat my mother ass and mine too last night." Come on, what the fuck dream world she living in? If she think the police bout to come up in my crib and do something just cause my daddy beating up on us, she a lot stupider than she should be if she went to law school. Maybe they come in Westchester or Long Island or Queens, but they ain't coming in Harlem. I would have to knock some white lady in the head and then drag her uptown to my crib and let her call the police from there if I wanted them to come and help me. I know I shouldn't have done it Natasha, but I couldn't help it. She made me so fucking mad I didn't know what to do. I wanted to kill her. I really did. I wanted to jump over my seat and grab her by the back of the head and put her in my mother's face and show her the scars that's still there and say, Look at this bitch. How would you like this every day bitch? But I knew I couldn't. I tried to be calm, but I couldn't help getting mad. I felt my face getting hot

*and sweat coming on my face and pouring down my face
and I just couldn't help it. I had to get mad. I had to. I
tried not to, but I couldn't help it. I fucked up baby. Please
don't be mad at me.*

    Love,
    Antonio

■

May 3, 1990
Dear Antonio,

Don't be mad at yourself. Things happen. I really didn't
think it was that bad. I mean, I could tell you was getting mad and you wanted to bust the bitch in her grill,
but you wasn't *that* mad. I've seen you really mad, like
when you all lost that basketball tournament at Riverside Church by like two points, and when your mother
told you that you couldn't be in the band no more cause
she couldn't afford to rent the drums anymore. Now you
was mad then, punching the walls and everything. But I
think you kept it together up there today. I guess we'll
see. Just between me and you, I don't think that the
other side is doing too good. It seem to me that the
lawyer lady who's against you is not very nice, and I
think the jury see that. Remember when me and you had
legal studies together and we learned all about the tactics
that lawyers is supposed to use in the courtroom? Remember when we talked about them being sensitive to

the jury, not alienating them and making themselves sympathetic? Dawg, I can't believe I remember all that. I probably should think about being a lawyer. Well anyway, I don't think she doing that right now. Like, when your lawyer gets up and say funny stuff or make little comments some of the jurors might laugh or smile, but they never do that with her. So see, that's a good sign. I don't know what I'm gonna do for the rest of the week, until we find out what they say. They gonna let you off, I know it. I can feel it in my heart. They can't deny the truth. They can't deny everything your mother said, all the good stuff people said about you, what the experts said about you defending yourself. Mommy said that she gonna come to the courthouse with me when the jury come back. Mrs. Lawrence said she gonna call me as soon as your lawyer call her, and we all gonna go down there together.

My grandma even said that she been praying for you Antonio. And my grandmother is a holy woman. I mean she don't smoke, she don't drink, she don't cuss, she don't dance unless she in church. She said Granddaddy the only man she was ever with in her whole life. Just like I'm gonna be with you, you gonna be the only man I'll ever let love me like that. But she said that at her prayer meetings on Wednesdays, they been praying for you Antonio. Her and a bunch of holy women like her. I been to their prayer meetings before. All the times I ran away to live with her, she made me go to church. She made me go to the prayer meetings with her. All the women look just like my grandmother—their skin shiny smooth and dark like the sky at night, gray hairs on their chins, bodies that look like men from behind, but when they turn around you see their breasts and stomachs so big from having so many kids. They don't even talk really at the meetings. Sing and pray. Sing and pray. That's all they do. When you walk through the door everybody singing without music and you just join in and start singing too. Then the oldest ones start praying and shouting and screaming and crying and they don't stop until everybody is sweaty and tired. They doing all that for you Antonio, probably while I'm writing this and while you reading it. So see, you got my grandma and her church, me and my mother, your family, the teachers at school, our friends. You got all these people pulling for you and all of us together can move a mountain. Where there's a will there's a way. We all can't be wrong.

Love,

Natasha

May 3, 1990
Dear Natasha,

My lawyer talked to me today. He asked me if I wanted to make a plea. I asked him why and he said that things wasn't looking too good. The biggest problem, aside from the fact that I blew my testimony, was that they went through my desk at school and found my notebook—you know the one Mr. Cook gave me with Malcolm X on the front. Remember when the prosecution showed them all the drawings I did when I couldn't concentrate in class cause my mind was on what was going on at home—pictures of me choking my father, stabbing him, pointing a gun at his head. They even found one part where I was supposed to be taking algebra notes but instead I was writing down how I was gonna shoot my daddy with a gun from Black's cousin. I tried to tell him that all of that was just make-believe, but he said it looked very real under the circumstances. I showed him your letters, and told him that you thought things was going cool and that things might go my way. He said that you wasn't a good judge of what was going on because you was biased. Remember we learned about bias in legal studies? Just in case you forgot, that mean you was on my side naturally cause you knew me. But he said that in his opinion, the way I acted on the stand hurt me. It hurt me real bad. He said that things was going great when I cried in front of them and everything, but he said that I was too hostile on the stand. He said that I came across as too angry, not apologizing for what I did, and like it was natural for me to do something like that again. I didn't think I was that bad, but he told me that I should think about pleading to involuntary manslaughter. He said that's a much lesser charge, and that I won't get as many years as if I was to get convicted of first or second-degree murder. Plus, he said the judge might have some sympathy for me because of my age and what I been through. He could *intervene and not sentence me to a lot. I don't know what I should do. I don't have that much time. I think it would be better to plead guilty and hope the judge would have some mercy on me, right? MGD and Mookie both been in the joint before. They said that their juries weren't shit, even though it was a few black people on there, and then they said the judge threw the book at them. They said they wasn't trying to scare me. Just keeping it real with you, Youngblood, first time around you should know. Maybe with manslaughter he'll let me out when I'm 21. Maybe I won't have to be in there for no 15 or 20 years like if I get second degree. I don't know what to do. My lawyer telling me one thing, my mother saying I shouldn't. She don't believe that people would think I was wrong for what I did, but my mother can be a little cuckoo sometimes. Ma is one of those people who always wanna give others the benefit of the doubt, she always want to try to see the good in people and not believe that they can do evil things. That's why she wouldn't leave my daddy. But see, I know better. I know that some of those people would love nothing better than to send a little no-good nigger like me away for life. They wanna put me under the jail so they won't have to worry about their purses or their big old rings being snatched. One less thug to fuck up the world. I think my lawyer might be right. I think that if the jury don't like me, then it's no hope. Baby don't be mad with me, but I think I'm gonna plead guilty and see what happens.*

With love,
Antonio

May 5, 1990
Dear Antonio,

Please, listen to me real good, about pleading guilty. Please Antonio, I'm begging you not to do this to yourself, to us. I think you making a big mistake. I think you should wait and see what the jury gonna say. I think you should just wait and see. I know you worried. I know you scared. I know you think you gonna go away for years and years and years, but I really think that they can let you off. I really think everybody believed you. Remember when you first wrote to me and you asked me what I thought? If I thought you killed your daddy? Well, at first I did. I didn't want to tell you, but at first I thought you was wrong. I thought there was something you coulda done to change it, and I was mad at you for going away and leaving me. Then I said, well dawg, would Antonio do something to me if I make him mad? But maybe after going there and seeing you every day and hearing what everybody had to say about you, I don't blame you. I don't think you did nothing wrong. I promise I don't. I think you did all you could do. I think you are a wonderful, smart, beautiful, and brave person. I think you are a hero. Please, don't plead guilty to anything. Don't do this baby. Don't forget that you a hero. Write me back as soon as you get this.

Love,
Natasha

■

May 5, 1990
Dear Natasha,

Well baby, that's it. It's done. I told my lawyer that I didn't want to take the chance. That I wanted to cop a plea. I'm scared Natasha. I know that you don't think I get scared, that I put on this front for you and my boys. But I get scared too. I get nervous and everything too sometimes. And I'm telling you, baby, I ain't never been scared about anything in my whole life as I am about this. I'm gonna go ahead and take the plea. Involuntary manslaughter. 10 years. Upstate. It's done.

Yours truly, A

PART TWO

May 19, 1990
Baby Girl,

I'm cold. I'm so cold I can feel my bones inside of me, holding my body together. I want to pull them out one by one and rub them together like they taught us to do sticks in day camp at the PAL, make a fire inside of me to keep my body warm. I feel alone, like I'm on the outside of the world looking in. Like I'm in a rocket ship going to the moon, staring out of the cockpit window at the earth all pretty and blue and alive below me. I'm gonna die in here. I'm so alone, I'm gonna die.

The first day I got here, they shaved my hair. They cut it all off. You know how long me and my moms been trying to grow my hair? It was almost down to the middle of my back, and they cut it all off. I ain't had my hair cut, other than the ends, since I was in the fifth grade or something like that. They took everything else from me—my clothes, the pictures I had put up, my box of letters, my belt so now my pants sag, my shoelaces so I'm walking around tripping all over myself. They say they gonna give it back to me, but I don't believe em. They had to take a man's hair too? I felt like Samson in the Bible, you know the strongest man who had ever lived? His woman tricked him into cutting all his hair so his enemies could capture him and break him down.

See, and you thought I didn't know nothing about church. But that's what they did to me baby. They broke me down when they did that, robbed me, took my manhood. I didn't mind them making me squat and sticking their fingers up my ass as much as I minded them taking my hair. I remember cats coming from the clinic talking about the doctor doing that to them all the time. My turn just came up. It wasn't as bad as I thought it would be. I just blocked it out and it was over in a few seconds. But my hair, I can't never get that back. Ever. Well, at least not for a long time. When it gets to be more than a few inches, I gotta start braiding it. No fros or long ponytails in here. They worried about you hiding weapons or contraband in your hair, so you gotta show some scalp all the time. I can't call up Laniece the way I used to though to braid it. But I don't know if I'm gonna want nobody touching me in here, not even the barber they make you go to.

I miss MGD and Mookie. I miss them brothers a lot. They kind of looked out for me, like I was their little bro or something. I liked that, being the youngest one for a change. All my life, I felt like it was kind of my responsibility to look out for Tyler and Trevon. I was their big bro, the one they looked up to, the role model. I was God. Plus, I knew that if anything ever happened to my daddy, then I would automatically be the man of the house. So, in a lot of ways I never got to be the kid I wanted to be. I always felt like I was the one who had to help my mother with the cooking and the groceries and the laundry and defending the house and everything else. I always felt like a little man trapped inside a boy's body, like I couldn't fuck up. Maybe that's why I acted like a fool in school and started hanging out and shit. I don't know. In here though, I can't feel like a little man. I gotta feel like I can handle anything, like I can take anything a motherfucker wanna give me. I only seen a handful of whites—only about ten inmates total in my wing. But they still running things cause it's only a handful of us in blue. Most of the guards is white, mean, red-faced motherfuckers who talk like they ain't from New York. In here, black stick with black, Puerto Rican with Puerto Rican. Just like life. Everybody got they territory—imaginary lines in the mess hall, the showers, the phones, the yard. Separate but UNequal, just like life. It's a few exceptions to that rule, a few cats in here who go "that" way. But not too many.

After a day of analyzing me and shit, they decided I should go to a Level 2, medium security block. First few days, I just ate by myself. I walked around the yard by myself. I didn't talk to nobody. I pretended like I was deaf and dumb. I would nod my head and that was it. I was focused on maintaining the mental. I wanted everybody to think I was crazy so I could get my respect. So they think I'm one of them niggers who seem all quiet and innocent like, but who'll cut your throat in a minute if you make em mad. That's what I wanted people to think about me, just in case they was planning on trying to fuck with me. And nobody bothered me. They left me alone. Didn't try to kid with me. I know I promised you I never would, but I'm thinking about getting with a gang. If you ain't gotta squad when you come in, you don't get no props coming through the door. You gotta fight for that shit like your life depends on it, cause it does. So I don't want to, but I'm thinking I need some protection. Until then, I'll just keep being quiet and crazy.

We get up everyday at 6, lights out at 10. That's how it is in here. It's actually kind of boring up here. It's nothing like you see on TV. It's no fights, no beating up with the guards, no screaming and yelling against the bars like animals in cages. When we go out in the yard, or the rec room, people just kind of hang with the same two or three cats all the time. I'm glad it's not like that. I was really really scared at first about being here because I thought that's how it was gonna be.

It's two of us in my cell, which is really like a tiny room. Two grown niggaz and one toilet that's real low to the ground with a rusty-ass sink on it. I'll piss in there or whatever, but I won't do a number two. I can't do it. Not even when my stomach hurt so bad I think I'm gonna throw up. I just wait until it's time for the showers or the yards, and I get one of the guards to escort me to one of the bathrooms. There's no door on the stalls, but at least it's a space between them, and if nobody in there I don't have to worry about them smelling on me. I would be too embarrassed. Plus, the guards be too busy talking or reading a girlie book anyway to pay attention. But my cellmate act like he don't care, like it don't bother him. He blow up the spot every day, and I just act like I don't see it or smell it.

But in my cell is this spic named Benito and right next

to us is this cat named Mohammed. Benito real quiet and shy, like a little kid on they first day of school. But he try to conversate once in a while with me, mostly about music and shit on TV. He love to talk about girlz too. Claim he got all the mamis in Harlem riding his dick. When he do talk, it's mostly about pussy. He be telling me about some girl he been with, where he fucked her, exactly how he did it. He told me how he did it in Central Park, the Cloisters, the Bronx Zoo, the Times Square McDonald's. He told me to name a place in New York and he said he bet he would have done it there. I said Coney Island and he said Done. Then I said the Statue of Liberty and he said Done. I said my address and he said Done. Then we both started laughing. I shouldn't have been surprised then when I found out he was in here for raping somebody. But he don't seem like the type, cause he one of them shy, Puerto Rican boys with that thick curly hair. The kind of guy all the girls like, the type who don't have to pull the panties down cause they slip down for him. But then I guess he is obsessed with sex. I know he beats his stuff every night. He in the top bunk and I hear the covers moving back, you know, in that beat we make when we doing something. Sometimes I hear him making noise too, whispering Gloria or Laura or something like that. I don't know, maybe that's his girl and who he be writing letters to like I write to you.

Mohammed don't say shit to us when we talking about that stuff. He one of those Hebrew Israelite or Nation of Islam people. Him and Benito gotta love-hate thing, like a

old couple. They slide mirrors through the bars and stare at
each other's reflections and kick it once in a while. Other
than that, Mohammed don't speak much. He just read his
books and write in these notebooks and shit. He got a thousand books and notebooks, and Benito hold onto some of it
for him. Him and Benito got into it one time. The very first
day I got here, about all of Mohammed shit. They almost
went to blows, but the guards came over and settled the
shit. I told Mohammed I didn't care if he took my space.
They gave me my pictures and letters back. That's all the
stuff I got right now, barely enough to fill my property box.
I got my pictures on the wall, and my letters and stuff under my bed. I ain't trying to collect too much more than
that. This place ain't my home, so I'm not even gonna get in
that mind-set of making it all cozy. Mohammed claim he
ain't never done nothing wrong, he claim he ain't killed
nobody. He in here for armed robbery or something like
that, but he said it wasn't him and he was framed or
whatever. Well, regardless of what he says, he in here for a
very long time, and he said he trying to be on his best behavior so he can get out when his parole come up.

I'm sorry this letter so long baby. It's late at night and
I can't sleep. And I'm sorry it took me so long to write you.
The truth is honestly, and don't take this the wrong way, I
was trying not to think about you and your pretty face because I would tear up, I miss you so much. And the wrong
thing to do in a place like this is cry and seem soft. I ain't
spoken to my mother either. When I did call her, she cussed
me out for waiting so long. I tried to explain to her that I

didn't want to be calling all the time, running up the phone bill and being a burden on her. Daddy gone, so she got enough on her mind to do without paying for my collect phone calls. She told me that was the stupidest thing she ever heard me say, so I promised her I would call her twice a week right after Wheel of Fortune *cause I know she at home watching that and she'll pick up the phone. And baby, I promise I'll call you and write to you too. This is the last time I'll ever go this long without communicating to you. That's a promise.*

Well, I gotta wrap this up because it's almost time for roll call. The sun is almost up. I can tell cause the little bit of sky I can see through this tiny window is that electric blue color, so I only got about two hours left to sleep. Plus, I think Benito up there beating his shit again and I ain't trying to hear that. So, I'll write you later. Write me back soon baby.

Love,

Antonio

■

May 22, 1990
Dear Antonio,

The prom was Saturday at this real nice restaurant downtown, by Battery Park and the water. We could see the Statue of Liberty from the place cause it was on the twentieth floor or something like that. They had punch, cake, and stuff like chicken wings and meatballs and little hot dogs wrapped in dough. It was almost like a wedding. Everybody had a date but me. Well, probably not everybody, but that's the way it seemed to me. Me and Laneice both wore black and white. Her mother made our dresses. They were all long and Marilyn Monroe like with a lot of ruffles at the bottom. Mine was strapless and Laneice had spaghetti straps. We both had high slits going up the thigh. Her mother found both of us some polka-dot shoes and a polka-dot purse to match, and Mommy let me wear lipstick. Laneice daddy drove us to the prom in a nice black Lincoln cause you know he part owner of this car service. We got there in style, cause most people took the train. Laneice went with Black, if you can believe that shit. I knew they liked each other. I don't know why they was always pretending like they didn't. They danced with each other all night and he brought her cake and punch and they took pictures together.

Anyway, our friend Geraldine who live in Washington Heights with her sister and her sister boyfriend had a big party after the prom. Her sister mad cool. She got this long apartment like one long hallway, and you have to walk through one room to get to the other. She made us Jell-O shots and spiked Kool-Aid and that Spanish rice with barbecue. We listened to that Spanish music all night, which was nice cause it was something different for a change. Laneice said she wasn't going to give Black none, but I know she did. In the last room of the apart-

ment, that's where people was going to do it because nobody was walking through it. Sherry and Kyle went back
there, so did Noel and Belinda. I think Geraldine was
back there all night cause I never saw her and it was supposed to be her party. Laneice and Black was slow-
dancing and then I saw them walk back there with some
other people. I asked Laneice the next morning if they
did it, and she was like, "How the hell was he gonna get
it past all them ruffles Ma put on my dress?" I think Mrs.
Clark knew exactly what she was doing, making them
dresses like a damn leotard. But when she came out she
didn't have no pantyhose on anymore, so I think she lying. You know I didn't go back there with nobody. I
didn't even dance with nobody. I mean, people was asking me and everything, but I turned them down. I was in
the kitchen mostly with Geraldine sister, helping her
with the food and stuff. She talked to me about love,
about how her man got on her nerves and how love hurt
sometime. She showed me a picture of him and their
daughter. I asked her where he was and she said that he
was spending the night with his moms so she could plan
the party, but she said he missed her already cause he was
calling every ten minutes. They had a fight earlier, and
she said she couldn't wait for him to come home tomorrow so they could make up. Talking to her made me feel
a lot better.

Anyway, here's a picture of me in my prom dress. I
know my eyes look a little red, but that's because I was
crying just a little from missing you. But I have that big

pretty smile that I know you like. Make sure you put the picture up so you can look at me when you get lonely.

Love,
Natasha

■

May 25, 1990
Dear Natasha,

Baby, thank you so much for all the pictures. You look so good in your prom dress that I had to take your picture down. Benito was staring at it a little too hard and I didn't want him to be up there jacking off and thinking about you. So I put it under my pillow and I was looking at it every night before I went to bed, but I had to stop that because then I was wanting to beat my own meat after looking at it, and I ain't trying to go out like that. So now I look at it first thing in the morning so your pretty brown eyes can wish me a nice day.

So Laneice and Black done hooked up? I'm not surprised. He told me he thought she was fine. Member when we all went down to Times Square on that Friday night, the first night me and you had kissed after you slapped me for grabbing your ass? Well, I had told Black then that I wanted to talk to you and he said he wanted to talk to you too. I told him hell no, you was mine. He had to take Laneice. He said Laneice was too mean, and he was right.

That bitch is mean, always snapping her fingers and fighting and balling with the boys and getting mad over each and every point. But he thought she was cute. He called her chocolate and liked her dimples and dark lipstick. But then when he tried to hold her hand, she snatched it away and told him to keep his motherfuckin hands off her. So it was a wrap. But I guess they finally found a common ground. I hope it work out for them a little better than it seem to be working out for us, though I'm still glad I didn't let him talk to you that night.

On another note, I finally got to take a shit in my own toilet. I got the cell all to myself. Benito and Mohammed was in the hole. Mohammed was just bugging out in our cell right after mess hall. Benito got mad cause on his bed Mohammed had left one of his headwraps or kente cloths or whatever that shit he got permission to wear on his head cause of his religion. So he went loco on Mohammed, talking about how he was sick and tired of Mohammed acting like he own the world and he know it all and shit. Then Mohammed said, I should be the one mad cause I gotta put this on my head and it's gone swimming in your cum. Then Benito decked him and Mohammed decked him back and before you know it everybody on the block was screaming and shouting and clanging shit up against the bars and the guards was running as fast as they could to get up here. Mohammed was telling Benito he was gonna fuck him up and Benito was saying the same, and I thought they really was gonna kill each other. Mohammed had Benito in a headlock, and Benito had started to breathe real funny and hard cause he couldn't catch his breath. Then he had elbowed Mohammed in the jaw, and I heard Mohammed neck snap back and he got real dizzy and fell. Then Benito had Mohammed head in the toilet. I didn't know what to do Natasha. All of the shouting and banging and shit, all of the sweat and noise and chaos in the room. This funny horn started going off, and then these bright white lights started flickering real fast like when you at the club. I got dizzy myself and I just got scared that all these people was gonna swarm in our cell and think I was fighting and then try to attack me too. So I covered my head and tried to crawl under my bed in the corner. I just crawled under there and I was shaking and crying and trying to cover my ears and shut my eyes and disappear. I saw the guards feet when they came in, and I heard the little sticks they carry thudding up against Benito and Mohammed. I heard one of them say, Where's the other one? Then hands was pulling my feet from under the bed. I thought they was gonna carry me away too, but they didn't. They just kind of grabbed me by the back of my neck and threw me on the bed and told me to get out of the way, which is what I was tryin to do before they pulled me from under the bed. Then they just took Benito and Mohammed away, while everybody on the block was spitting and yelling and cussing out the guards. I saw our door slide back and I heard that click to let me know I was locked in, then I knew I was safe. Then I knew that nobody was gonna take me away too or swarm the cell and deck me too. Things had been cool up to

*this point. It hadn't been no drama, but I hope that I never
have another day like this again as long as I'm in here.*

    Stay safe,
    Antonio

■

May 30, 1990

Antonio baby, I'm so sorry you had to go through what
you went through and I wasn't there so you could lay
your head on my shoulder and I could make you feel all
better. I could hear it in your voice the other day when
you called that you wasn't doing too good. Something
was weird, like you wanted to tell me something but
couldn't find the words or get it out. Now I know what it
was. You was scared baby, and that's okay. I wish that I
could talk to you and call you or you call me so I could
calm you down whenever you get upset like that, but I
can't. Roy said something to Mommy about you calling
here. He said that if I wanted to talk to you I needed to
get a job and pay for the calls myself. Well, you know
what? That's exactly what I'm gonna do. I'm seventeen
now. I can get a real job. I want to go and work at the
Macy's downtown so I can get a discount, or one of them
stores on 5th Avenue so I can buy myself a lot of clothes
and save up some money to go to college and get my own
place and get the hell out of this house. So Antonio, I'm
sorry I have to say this, but I don't think you can call

here anymore. It's not that I don't want to talk to you, it's just that I don't want to make Roy mad because I don't want him and Mommy fighting. It's been real good around here. They haven't been fighting, Drew been coming around. We even went downtown to see a Eddie Murphy movie the other day. So the last thing I want to do is cause some trouble over a phone bill. When I get my job I'm gonna get my own phone line, then you can call as much as you want.

Love you forever,
Natasha

■

June 7, 1990
Natasha,

Well baby I know I promised you I wouldn't, but I got in trouble already. The other day I had met with this woman who come to the spot once every two weeks. They call her the Education Coordinator. She an older black lady named Ms. Harris. She's not really that much older, only maybe thirty or something. The cats on the block told me her first name was Dream. I thought they was joking, but they said that her name really was Dream but it should be Wet Dream, cause every time after she come visit, everybody need to have their sheets washed cause they been thinking about her all night. She's pretty, kinda remind me of you, a little bit of Janet Jackson when she was on Different Strokes *back in the day. She ain't nearly as fine as you though before you start tripping. She just real nice and sometimes that can make the ugliest person look beautiful. It's mandatory for all the new inmates, although I hate calling myself that, to meet with Ms. Harris when they first come in. She was like, Antonio I see from your file that you're only seventeen years old, you're just a baby. I told her, Miss, no disrespect, but after all I been through in my life I ain't no baby. She didn't get mad though. She just said real cool and sassylike, Didn't mean to disrespect you brother. Now ain't nobody who wasn't really my brother ever called me that, so she got my attention real quick with that one. She just said, I didn't mean to imply you're too young or too inexperienced or that you weren't an adult in this case being a baby is a good thing because you have a lot of time to fulfill your educational goals.*

Now Natasha, I had never thought about having any educational goals other than getting my diploma until I met you and decided I needed to do better with my life. So I didn't say nothing for a minute and then finally I was like, I thought about being a scientist. Just cause I had told you that before and I thought it sounded good. I mean going to see Ms. Harris is a privilege, not a right. You can't have no points against you, and you have to be serious cause the first thing she told me when I met her was: Hi, I'm Ms. Harris, I'm here to help you and if you don't want my help leave now and don't waste my time. She thought that was real cool Natasha that I wanted to be a scientist, cause she was real interested and she wasn't being fake about it. She asked me what kind of scientist I wanted to be. I didn't know it was different types, so I just said a regular scientist. You know all scientists make STUPID dough, I told her. She said, I mean do you want to focus more on physics or chemistry or biology or agriculture or astronomy? I thought about some of the things we had did in Mrs. Jensen's class, like putting plastic tight over a jar of peanut butter and watching it swell up with air pressure and all that. Ms. Harris said, That sounds a little like chemistry and physics you're interested in the secrets of the universe how things react to one another and how different forms of life interact and coexist. Now I didn't know what the hell she was trying to say. I guess I do, I mean I am interested in that type of shit but not in a scientific way. Like I'm interested in how the hell anybody could expect for me and my family to coexist with somebody like my daddy was, or how white people think they can live in the world and never interact with us unless we doing something for them. But I didn't say that. I just told her she was right. So then she was like, Antonio I think that's great and I think you can definitely accomplish at least some of that goal while you're in here but the first step for you is to get your GED. I told her that I didn't want no damn GED cause a GED was for stupid people. Then I caught myself cause I remember that she was a nice lady, somebody who I can't disrespect. She was like, Antonio, GED stands for general equivalency diploma and it is a perfectly legitimate way for people whose circumstances have prevented them from finishing high school to obtain their diploma. Far from being a sign that you're stupid it is a sign of empowerment because it shows that you want to take control of your life and your future. I told her that I was going to go back to high school because the judge who sentenced me was going to have a change of heart and let me out. She said, Antonio, it says in your file that you pleaded guilty to involuntary manslaughter in order to get a reduced sentence and that means you have no appeals, which means your only hope of getting out of here will come when your sentence is up in about ten years. I told her she was wrong and that I was gonna get out. She picked up my file again and said, But look here Antonio, your file says . . . Then I said, Fuck the file, and I snatched it from her hands and threw it across the room and then I threw my chair across the little tiny office we was in and then I knocked all the stuff off the desk with one hand.

The last thing I saw before three of them big guards came and wrestled me down on the ground and put their knees in my back was Dream face, it was all twisted and scared and I think she was about to cry. I fucked up Natasha and I don't think she'll want to see me again. I had to meet with the warden, and he told me that already I hadn't been there but a month and I was fucking up and he thought I was different from the rest of the trash they get and now he was gonna have his eye on me. I had to spend three days in solitary. It really wasn't that bad. It wasn't like you see on TV with somebody stuck down in a little hole with nothing but bread and water. I was just in a tiny room with no bars, just a little slit in the door where

they passed my food and stuff. You couldn't talk to nobody
through the doors or the walls cause they was too thick. You
couldn't do nothing really but sit on the floor and think
and stare at the white walls. That's what I did every day.
I just stared and stared and stared until they let me out
this morning.

   Love,
   Antonio

■

June 14, 1990
Dear Antonio,

Antonio, I feel like so far I been real supportive of you
and everything you been going through. But I just have
to tell you that what you did was real stupid Antonio. It
was just stupid and dumb and how do you expect them
to let you out of there early if you wanna go and attack
the staff? I mean I can't believe you did that and got
yourself in trouble. That's gonna go in your file Antonio,
I hope you know that. That's gonna go in your file and
it's gonna be on your record permanently as a sign of
what you did and how you act when you get privileges.
This woman Ms. Harris was right. You do need your
GED right now. It's no point in sitting in there waiting
to get out when you can be getting that and moving on
with your life and going to college. Now they probably

not gonna even let you go to college or go to the GED classes or nothing. Well, I'm telling you this, Antonio, I'll stick by you and be your woman and support you and all that, but I ain't marrying no bum. That's what my mother did with Roy. Get with some man who can't do shit for her but give her some dick and dick don't pay the bills. That's what she says all the time to me: "Natasha, dick don't pay the bills. Get a man with a job and some education." That's what I'm gonna do, Antonio. Now, you can be that man or you can get yourself in trouble. It's up to you. But I'm not gonna sit around and think about you and pay for your phone calls and write you all these letters if you just gonna go and get yourself in trouble.

I might as well tell you now cause I was gonna surprise you, but you need to know right now. I got into that special program that Madame Girard had me apply to. It's called a French immersion program and I got in because of my recommendations and my essay and my B average. This summer, I'm going to go to Paris. Me. Natasha Riley. I'm going to France, a whole other country in the universe, far away from Harlem and New York City and New York State and America period. On Saturday I went to the special orientation for the program. I used my discount from Macy's to buy myself a nice little red sweater and some black dress pants and some shiny black shoes with a little heel so I could look nice and like I was serious, not there to play games. It was at Hunter College and I was the only person there from my school. It was mostly black and Spanish kids, but there was some Chinese and Indian people. They had sandwiches and chips and soda and everything for us. I met two girls that I think I'm gonna be tight with, this thick girl from Brooklyn named Tamika James and this real tall Dominican chick named Valencia Vasquez who live uptown too. Valencia dressed from head to toe like she about to ball, and Tamika told her, "Mami, you gotta put on something way better than that if you spect them to take you serious." And Valencia was like, "I dress like this so people can take me serious. I gets mad respect this way, I get disrespected when I look like a girl. This is me and whoever don't like it fuck em." It look like Tamika was bout to say something smart and I kind of jumped in to clarify what Tamika had said. I don't think she was making fun of Valencia or anything. I think she was just trying to tell her what people like Mr. Cook always told us: "You gotta dress for success." So I just said, "Well, it don't look like it's too many of us here and trying to go somewhere in life so we gotta dress proper so we can represent." Valencia just nodded her head and played with this cross around her neck and chewed on one of her long braids like, "Yeah, I guess you right. I guess you got a point. But I still ain't wearing no dress though." From that point on, it was all love. I think we gonna be good friends. This black man started out talking to us in French, and he told us we had to just figure out what he was saying before we could eat. Then he started laughing and told us he was joking and started talking about the program in

English to us. It was some other white people with him and they all started the program together. He told us that we would get help with our French and extra tutoring in other subjects in school. Then, in our senior year they help us apply to college and give us special classes for the college entrance exams we have to take. I showed my mother all the stuff we was gonna do and she told me how proud she was of me, and how since I was doing that she was gonna get off her butt and apply for that house. So see, Antonio, I'm going places with my life and I love you and want to be with you, but you gotta keep it together. Like everybody told me after my daddy died and I started acting up, this ain't the time to be feeling sorry for yourself. And really it's not. Now the first thing you need to do is apologize to Ms. Harris. You need to write her a letter and see if you can come back. You need that GED Antonio, and anything else they gonna give you so when you get out we can both have our shit together. Don't write me or call me until you write that letter to Ms. Harris. I mean it Antonio.

Natasha

■

June 17, 1990
Dear Ms. Harris:

First of all, I want to start out by apologizing for what I did in your office. I'm real sorry about that and it won't happen *again if you decide to see me again. I know you just trying to help us and I really appreciate you trying to help us. I'm sure you could be anywhere in the world you want to be because you seem like a nice person with a lot of education. So the fact that you come here and see us is a good thing and we should appreciate it and not waste your time like you said. But my girl kinda helped me realize why I did what I did and some of the stuff that I'm feeling. I think I was kind of feeling sorry for myself about being in here and what's happened to me. I think I was mad because it happened and I wanted somebody else to take the rap. The truth is, and I wish I would've said this when I had the chance and when it mattered. But the truth is, I am really sorry for what I did and I wish I would not have been so mad and not thinking straight that day. The other truth, ~~Dream,~~ I mean Ms. Harris, is that I really miss my daddy. You know what I did because I know you have my file because I snatched it out of your hands. But I miss my father and I am so so so so sorry for what happened. He did things that were really bad to me and my brothers and my mother, but he really wasn't that bad to get what he got, or what I gave him because now I'm accepting the blame. But what I wish I would have done was just leave the house and take my family with me and leave my father alive so he could grow up and change. Then in the future we all could have came together and had our differences settled because we would be grown and he wouldn't have that same power over us that he had before. That's what I wish. But we did some things together like he taught me how to ride a bike and we used to stay up late at night and watch*

TV sometimes and he would cook stuff like steak and eggs or popcorn in the skillet and we would watch stuff like Columbo and Kojak real late and he would ask me sometimes about school or about the honey who he was seeing come around the house. That's the daddy I try to remember and that I cry about when I know nobody is listening or watching. So that's where I'm coming from. I think you're right and my girl right. I do need my GED and I want to meet with you to talk about how we can do that. I'm gonna give this note to somebody to give to you because I don't trust the guards to do shit for me. I hope you get it and put my name on the list for an appointment with you. Once again, I'm sorry. Please accept my apology.

Sincerely,

Michael Antonio Lawrence II

PS. My number is 007624 in case you forgot Natasha, now you happy? Write back.

PSS. Happy birthday. The last thing I want to be is locked up in here on your birthday. I dreamed I bought you something nice, a diamond tennis bracelet or something. Then we went on a cruise somewhere nice and laid up on the beach all day. That's what you deserve for your birthday. That's what I wish I could have gave you.

June 21, 1990
Antonio,

Thank you for the birthday wish. Me and Mommy and
Laneice and Drew and Grandma went to Red Lobster in
the Bronx. I love Red Lobster. They got the best biscuits.
Mommy had told me I could pick a lobster which was
crazy cause she ain't never said that cause lobster is mad
expensive. But she was like, "Go ahead, it's your birthday." So I was gonna go ahead and do it, but when I saw
them climbing all around on top of each other, smashed
together in that tiny tank, those rubber bands on their
hands like handcuffs, for some reason I don't know why I
just thought about you and I couldn't pick one. I had
fried jumbo shrimp instead. Laneice got me this real nice
stationery set and some perfume, and Mommy and
Grandma got me a gold locket with my daddy picture
inside. I swear I'm gonna wear it all the time and never
take it off.

Okay, you right, that's a really good letter and I hope
she put your name on the list for that appointment. I'll
keep my fingers crossed for you. I think she will. One
thing about us black women is we forgive our men too
much for the shit you do. Least that's what my mother
say all the time. So you miss your daddy, baby? How
come you never told me that? So see now, that's another
sign we was meant to be together cause it means we have
something in common. We both miss our daddies. It's

kind of really sad if you think about it, that our kids won't have no real grandfathers, only grandmothers. That make me think about this article I read in *Essence* and I tried to translate into French for that program I'm in. Basically, the article talked about how it was a black male crisis in our community because of prisons and early average death age for black men and stuff. They was talking about how black men are going to prison more than college. This woman named Angela Davis who used to be a Black Panther was interviewed for the article. Remember I told you about her and how my mother said the popo's had busted into her apartment when she was little because her big sister Ruth was tall and skinny and lightskinned with a big Afro? Well, the FBI was looking for this woman Angela Davis and somebody had gave an anonymous tip that Angela Davis was living in that apartment. Well, looking at this picture this woman don't look nothing like Aunt Ruth but guess from a distance she could.

Hey, Laneice and Black been kickin it real tight lately. They be together all the time and all she talk about is Black Black Black Black. I'm so sick and tired of hearing about Black I don't know what to do. "Black bought me some sneaks, Black took me to KFC, Black took me to the new scary movie, Black Black Black Black." She think he love her, but it seem to me that all he want to use her for is sex. Every time I look up they bumpin and grindin or getting ready to—in the movie theater, in the stairway at school. I mean, she was giving him head in the middle of that new Jason movie at the 14th Street theater. And this chick with a big old Afro and these thick glasses had went and told the usher and we got kicked out. It was just the matinee so it was only five dollars, but still. I told my grandmother about it cause I went up to her place when we got out cause I DID NOT feel like hanging with them no more. My grandmother said, "That's nasty and disgusting and I hope you're not out there behaving like a heathen." I told her, "No, Nana, I'm not." She still think I'm a virgin. I feel like one now that you ain't around. That's why I don't want to hear Laneice personal bizness all the time. I don't even want to go nowhere with her no more cause we somehow always end up at Black spot or with Black. And the other night she musta lied to her mother and said she was spending the night at my house and didn't tell me nothing, cause Mr. Clark called over here for her. That bitch is lucky I answered the phone and was able to lie and tell him that she was in the shower. Then the first place I called was Black house cause I knew that's probably where she was, and sure enough that's where she was cause his mother had went down to Virginia to see her sister. I told her, "Bitch don't be using me for no cover and then not telling me." That's a lotta nerve. She told me she was sorry and I guess she called her father or whatever. But anyway I told her she better be careful if she don't want to get pregnant. She had basically let it slip that sometimes they don't even be using nothing and he just pull it out. I told her she was stupid. Now me and you ain't never did that. We was always safe and I told her that she had to be if she wanted to go to college and be somebody.

But honestly Antonio, when she be talking about her and Black being together, and one time when I was at her house and her parents wasn't there and he came over and they did it and I heard them doing it, I thought about us and I just had to play with myself down there. I know it's wrong and it's not like the real thing, but I just had to cause I thought I was gonna bust into a thousand little pieces if I didn't. Antonio, I wish it was some way I could see you. I miss you baby. Do you miss me? Don't you think about me and being with me? It's been now about six months since we did something, remember we did it at your house that one night when we came back from the movies and your mother was sleep in her room and your father was out and we did it on the couch real slow and quiet for a long time so the couch wouldn't squeak? You was real good that night. I had got in trouble for coming home late, but I didn't care cause you made me feel so good. Well, I need you to make me feel good again, but the only problem is I'm here and you there and we can't be together until you get parole so I'm gonna have to just wait and be a virgin all over again.

Laneice said that if you and me both kind of think about each other at the same time, like say around midnight or whatever, and if we both touch ourselves in that way we both like at the same time, then that's just the same as doing it. So, why don't we do that on Thursday?

We'll do that together and it'll be just like we making love.

Love always, your one and only,

Natasha

■

June 24, 1990
Natasha,

Yeah baby girl I thought about you real hard last night. I thought about your pretty caramel skin and them nice juicy lips always taste so sweet and that big phat ass you got and your little titties that so nice and tight and I thought about you not just at midnight like you said but all night. I especially thought about them times when we was alone like at my uncle house when he had went to Mexico with his girlfriend and he left me the keys cause he said he know sometimes a man wanna be alone with his woman. I thought about how we got to take off all our clothes those times and how we was able to make as much noise as we wanted and how I was able to do it to you over and over again real hard and make you scream my name real loud til you couldn't scream no more and you just started whispering it cause we was so sweaty and tired. That was the best time we did it and I thought about it all night. I came like twice thinking about you. Did you come thinking about me? I hope you did over and over again until you wanted to scream my name but you just had to whisper it cause peo-

ple was in the house. You know, Benito and Mohammed came back. First they was on different blocks cause of the fight and everything, but then they couldn't get along with the new mates so they just shook hands and came right back to where they were. But I wish I woulda had the whole place to myself cause I didn't like jacking off like Benito, but I had to do what I had to do for real. I was telling Mohammed about you and he said that we could get married if we wanted to. Then, maybe next year or whatever depending on my behavior, you could come visit me for like two days or whatever and we could be alone. They give you a trailer and all you gotta do is come out and show your face every two hours. I think there's a camera or something to make sure we ain't doing nothing illegal but baby don't worry I can make you forget all about a camera. Try to come this weekend with my mother. Try to come up here so I can see you. I need to see you so bad. I miss you baby.

Love,
Antonio

■

July 3, 1990
Antonio,

Thank you so much for my ring!!!! It's so pretty and shiny and bright and when I flick it under the fluorescent lights in the auditorium at City College I can see a million colors! Thank you thank you thank you baby! The whole way up there on the bus to see you Mrs. Lawrence kept on looking at my hands and picking them up talking about "Girl, you got big hands. You got man hands." Now that I look back she had that ring in her purse to give me and she was nervous it wasn't gonna fit. Then Tyler kinda let it slip cause he said something like "It's too big, Ma" and then she popped him the mouth and he didn't do shit but stare out the window until we got there. I wish you coulda been on one knee to give it to me and I could have kissed you like I was supposed to, but it's kind of impossible to do that between all that glass, I understand. But it was still nice. I told my mother all about it, and she just kind of looked at me and shook her head and said, "Oh my God." I don't care if she ain't happy about it. It's my decision and I'm gonna do what I'm gonna do. I think she just jealous cause I got a diamond that stick out big and far on my finger, and all she got is a little tiny glass chip in her ring from Roy.

Don't think I ain't been showing everybody. It was a big b-ball game on Sunday at Rucker and it was a lot of people there from my old crew. They all was looking at me all jealous like, talking bout "She think she the shit cause she got a piece of ice on her finger." They said that shit under they breath cause they knew better than to say it out loud. Specially since I was sitting with Laneice and Black, and Black's cousin Demonte who just got out the joint and don't care nothing bout cutting nobody throat.

He had on his skully, smoking a Black and Mild and looking all scary with that big razor scar down his cheek coming down to his chin. They looked over at us and just kept on whispering cause they know what's good for em. I just ignored them females cause I'm above all that, Antonio. These bitches still on some childish he-say she-say I gotta get my hair and nails done shit. I'm moving on from that and growing up. That's why I like Tamika and Valencia so much, because they both got goals and trying to do something with they life that's beyond the everyday shit people tell us we can do. I gotta keep on studying hard and doing my thing so I can get picked to go to France, and saving up all the money I make at Macy's so I can get my own place when I get ready to go to college.

I been saving all my money. I ask Mommy if she need anything and she always say no, so I just go and buy groceries and toilet paper and hair stuff cause she won't take my money. I'm taking Drew school shopping at the end of the summer so he won't be going to school looking all raggedy. I got the clothes, it's on Grandma to keep his hair cut. Other than that, I ain't wasting my money on no juvenile shit like hair and nails and fake Gucci purses and niggaz who ain't doing shit for me. But you love me, Antonio, and I know you gonna take care of me when you get the chance. I'm gonna send you some money so you can get snacks and other stuff you wanna buy with your money. You can save it or do whatever you want with it. I don't care. I just want you to know I got your back cause I know when the time come you gonna have mine.

Love,

Natasha

■

July 10, 1990
Natasha,

Thank you for the package of stuff you sent me. I needed all of it so much—the toothbrushes, the socks, underwear. I liked the body soap and loofah sponge even though it was girlie. You remembered my Cheetos and Doritos too, didn't you? I had to sit there and wait for them to open every single thing and search it for contraband. They dumped all the shampoo and body wash and chips and put it in these plastic bags. I wanted to go loco cause they didn't have a right to open shit I didn't even want to open yet, but I just held my tongue cause I don't want to jeopardize my right to get a package next quarter. Contraband gets in and that's all there is to it. They can't stop that shit. I seen more drugs in here than I seen in my whole life on the outside. Weed, crank, speed, crack—all that shit somebody done tried to push on me, in the yard mostly cause everybody out in the open and guards ain't right up on you. But me and my cellmates ain't interested in that shit. Mohammed too righteous for it and Benito's only drug is pussy. I just don't wanna go out like that. Dogs come search our cells all the time—in the middle of the night, while your wing is out in the yard. The point is to catch us off guard. And they find shit too. They found five bags of heroin inside a radio of this cat on our wing last time, plus bout five Gs he had saved up from dealing. Mohammed claim the real people they need to be searching is the guards and the rest of the staff. He got a point. As much shit as I know is coming through here, dealers inside gotta be getting some help.

Don't get offended and don't take this the wrong way but I'm sending your money back because I'm a man and I can't take no money from my woman. Even Mohammed was like, That's not cool son. Black women got it hard enough without trying to take care of us. And he right. Mohammed kinda weird and a little nerdy but he can kick some knowledge when he want to. I just don't want my woman sending me money that's all. So I'm gonna send it back. Pretty soon, I'm gonna be eligible to get a job here, maybe in the kitchen or the library or the laundry. In a few years, I might even move up to Wall Street—that's what cats call the woodworking factory cause you get to make shit. You get to use your hands and tools and creativity on some level to make all these little wooden parts that they ship out to factories across the country. But that's for the old timers and the nonviolent cats. But it's exceptions based on your behavior and I do plan on keeping my shit together once I start studying again. So I'll be alright and make my money without you thinking about me. Keep it and buy something real nice and send me a picture so I can see it.

Love,

Antonio (your man)

July 11, 1990
Antonio,

Well, Antonio, I am a little bit upset you didn't take the money. That was something I wanted to do for you as a present. People give each other presents all the time. That's all it was. But if you feel like I'm disrespecting on your manhood then I can't do nothing but respect that. But I'm telling you, if you need it, don't be afraid to ask.

One person I ain't giving no money to is Roy. Now lemme tell you what this nigga did. He gonna ask me to go to the corner store right and pick him up some stuff. He was smoking the joe and got the munchies, plus he wanted some cigarettes and you remember Sanchez who own the store? Well, he always let me buy cigarettes for Mommy and Roy cause he know us. So I went and got just what Roy asked for: some Newports, OJ, cheese popcorn, 7Up, and we needed some more dish soap. So I'm thinking he gonna give me the money before I left, but he claimed he was gonna give it to me when I got back. Well, when I came back he gonna talk about "Well if you had the money anyway it's no use in me giving it back to you." So I started screaming that I wasn't giving him his shit and he was like, "Girl you better quit playing with me. I ain't yo mama." And I wasn't gonna give it to him Antonio, I meant it. But then my mother came out her room cause she was in there under the hood dryer wrapping her hair, and usually she don't take my side so

I just threw the bag on the floor and stomped to my room to turned on Queen Latifah just like I always have to. On the way back there though my mother said, "Roy, that's Natasha's money. If I don't ask her for it then neither should you." And Roy screamed "Denise, she need to contribute to this house. She grown and old enough to open her legs and hit the streets when she wanna so she shouldn't be hollering about no damn ten dollars." Now, Antonio that made me so mad cause compared with most kids my age, I'm doing good with myself. I don't even go out that much, only to the movies or parties or Times Square and that's only on the weekend. So my mother said, "Natasha do her part with the chores and she pay for almost everything she want, so I don't ask her for no money and she my own daughter." Then Roy was like, "Oh she my daughter too when the rent need to be paid to keep a roof over her head, but she your daughter when it's time to correct her?" Then Mommy said "You ain't correcting her—you just keeping up mess." Then I just heard Roy stomping around and opening the front door and he said something out in the hall like, "This whole house ain't nothing but a mess. Drew had some sense getting the hell out."

Well he was gone for a while before my mother came in the room with a towel wrapped around her head and she sat on my bed I guess expecting me to say something, but I just looked at her like, "What?" And she said, "Natasha, can't you just try to stop fighting with Roy? Y'all driving me up the wall, I swear." And I didn't even feel like talking about it, so I just sighed real loud and then she kept looking at me and I was like "What?" again. And she said, "Well, girl answer me," and I said, "I didn't know there was a question," and she just said, "Watch your mouth." I just told her, Antonio, that I didn't like him, matter of fact I hated him and I couldn't wait to leave and I was going to France and not coming back. Then I told her about Laneice's mother and father, about how they didn't scream and fight and holler all the time and that was why I liked to go over there so much. I expected my mother to say something to that, but she didn't for a while and when I finally looked up she had her head down and she was crying. I didn't know what to do, so I just started crying too and I hugged her and told her I was sorry. She just said, "Natasha, when your father died I didn't know what I was gonna do. I really didn't, especially since we had nowhere to go. Roy came along and made me feel like a woman again and it had been so long." Then she kind of embarrassed me cause she said, "I know Antonio make you feel like a woman, that's why you love him so much. I ain't stupid." Then I said, and I wasn't trying to be smart, Antonio, I really wasn't, "Is that a question?" She didn't get mad though, she just got up and said, "I don't ask questions when I already know the answer cause that's a waste of God's time." Then she turned off my light like she used to do when she tucked me in the bed and before she walked out she told me, "I know you miss your daddy. I miss him too."

Then I was in the dark all by myself, swallowed up by

the black night, swallowed up by a floating lonely, swallowed up by deep down dark that's inside you and not just around you and likes to tease you and say look at me I'm here and I ain't goin nowhere so you better get used to it.

Love your lonely girl,
Natasha

■

July 18, 1990
Hey There Lonely Girl! (You know that song,
*   don't you?)*

But anyway baby, don't feel like you alone. I wish I could say I feel you but I can't cause I have grown niggaz snoring all around me so I'm feeling quite crowded right now. But for real though baby girl, cheer up. I can't stand the thought of you feeling lonely. I can't live with it. And the reason why is because I know it's all my fault. I know it's on me why you alone, cause I ain't there to hold you or for you to call me on the phone and bitch about him. Tell you the truth, if I was there I would punch his ass for you, but I ain't there so I can't. Maybe it'll cheer you up to know that Ms. Harris answered my letter and she put my name on the list for an appointment with her. I ain't gonna give you the copy to read cause I wanna keep it since it's so nice and I keep all my letters to read when I'm bored or whatever, but here's what it say: "Antonio, I accept your apol-

ogy and understand why you may have acted the way you did. I was a little hurt by your actions, but it is not the first time something like that has happened to me and I'm sure it won't be the last. But you sound sincere in your letter, so with that maybe you and I can start fresh. Why don't we start our new beginning with you writing a book report for me? I want you to finish a book that you find interesting, and then write about it. You can write anything you want—a summary, response, critique, or review. This will help me assess your skill level and then decide where we should begin. I look forward to receiving that and seeing you again. Thank you again for your apology. Ms. Harris."

Now wouldn't you know that this same day I got this note, Mr. Cook came up here to see me? Come to find out, he got a nephew in the joint. I couldn't believe a man like Mr. Cook would know somebody here. Then again, he knows me. He said that he definitely wanted to see me in person so he could tell me not to give up on my dreams. I gave that cat hell in his class, but I guess he used to kids like me. I was surprised because normally we have to put all the people we expecting to come visit us on a list, but he said he had some connections. I'm wondering what kind of connections a man like Mr. Cook could have in the joint, but then again I guess you can't judge a book by its cover. I mean, the man did rap in class so maybe he a little bit tougher than we think. But anyway, he told me that he came to bring something that belonged to me. It was my copy of The Catcher in the Rye. He said that he had held on to it for me cause he had thought things might be dif-

ferent and I would come back to class. I asked him why he think to bring me the book, and he said I could tell that you liked it. I don't see how he could tell that since I flunked every quiz he gave us on it, but he is a really smart man I guess when it's all said and done. He said he couldn't stay that long cause him and his wife and kids was gonna see some family she had up in Connecticut, so he had to go cause he had left them at the IHOP to come see me.

I didn't do nothing all day Sunday but read that book again so I could write my report and get it to Ms. Harris so I could get in the class. I mean, it ain't no coincidence that he brought me the book and she wanted a report. That's a sign from the Most High as Mohammed put it that I gotta get it together, don't you think? I'm gonna write that report tomorrow, and I'm gonna do it all by myself. You remember how I used to always ask you to write my shit for me? Well, this time I'm gonna do it all by myself, with no help from anybody. I might ask Mohammed to look at it for spelling and puncutation, and that's it. I promise I'm not gonna disappoint anybody anymore.

Love,
Antonio

■

July 27, 1990

I'm sorry I took so long to write back to you, but I had to sort out some things I wanted to say to you. You know what Antonio, sometimes I feel like you don't even be listening to me or caring about what I have to say. I know you try to cheer me up, but I think you need to realize you ain't gotta be locked up to be lonely. I have a lot of problems and a lot of things I think about and want to do myself. It's like lately I been feeling your letters is all about you and you ain't interested in me no more. And I think you trying a little too hard to impress this Ms. Harris so I'm wondering if you got feelings for her. I saw your mother the other day and she told me you sent her the paper you wrote and all the good comments Ms. Harris had wrote on it, and I got a little bit upset cause you ain't said nothing to me about it. What, you got sumthin to hide? You need not be worried about Ms. Harris. You need to be worrying about your mother. Antonio, the truth is she don't look too good. She done put on a lot of weight I can tell you that. You ain't seen her in a while, but the next time you see her you'll see what I'm talking about. Now Mrs. Lawrence always had them hips, but it's like her stomach got big and her arms swelled up and every time I come over there she just sitting on that couch with a bowl of dried-up food on the front table, smelling up the room. She just flip channels over and over again, from Oprah to *People's Court* to *Days of Our Lives* to whatever. I keep asking her when she gonna go back to her job and she keep saying she ain't ready. Tell you the truth I think she fired and don't want to accept it or admit it. I don't know where Tyler and Trevon be half the time. It's the summer, so I guess they be out on the courts or riding bikes.

But anyway she took all Mr. Lawrence pictures down, and on Saturday me and her took the bus down to 125th to the Salvation Army to donate some of his clothes. I guess she finally accepting that he gone. Now, if you don't want her to take your pictures down and give your clothes away (starting with the kicks), you better start showing some concern for somebody other than yourself. Like about time I started thinking about myself for a change. I'm starting to turn out just like my mother, thinking about everybody else and not myself. Well, that's about to change. I'm going to France in less than a month and I asked for more hours so I could save up some money for my trip, so I'm not gonna have that much time to write. Go ahead and keep yourself busy with Ms. Harris while I handle my business.

Best wishes,

Natasha

■

July 31, 1990

First of all Natasha, no you do not know what it's like to be me. You do not know what I been through and what I go through every motherfucking day of my life. You don't have a clue what it's like to smell another man's shit or to be scared to look somebody in the face for fear you might get clocked for nothing or to have to do the same thing over and over every day at the same time every day or to have somebody watch you take a piss or wash your nuts. You don't know how heavy a dead body is and how no matter now hard you try you can't get that wide eye look out of your head and that soggy water smell out of your nose and the gargling noises it make when it's trying to breathe out of your dreams at night. So when you know all of that get back to me and criticize me and accuse me of not giving a fuck. And don't worry about my mother. I got that. Let me take care of that. You don't think I talk to her, you don't think I know what's going on? I don't need you to tell me shit.

    Antonio

PS. If I did like Ms. Harris (which I don't and I don't know where the fuck that came from) you ain't making it no better by going loco for nothing. She understanding me a little bit better than you are now so I hope you think about that while you enjoying your free life and trip to France. Suck my dick. I hope you was just on your period when you wrote that shit.

■

August 1, 1990
Dear Antonio,

Well, baby, you right. I guess I did fuck up. I was real mad when I read your letter and thought about giving you your ring back. I even told Laneice, "Fuck that nigga." But then I showed my mother and she explained to me that I might be a little bit insensitive. I don't know what you are going through and I don't know how it is for you. I was just a little bit upset and disappointed and worried that me and you wouldn't be able to be together. I'm just scared, Antonio. I'm really scared about us growing apart and not seeing each other. I don't know if I can handle it. I'm not saying I don't love you, I'm just saying that this is a lot for me too. I just need to know that you think about me the way I think about you. I need to know that you ain't gonna change and come out all hard and scarred up and painted from head to toe with nasty ass tattoos and shit. I see niggaz when they get out of lockup, some of my cousins or peeps from the block. And Antonio, they ain't the same. They meaner, more quiet, don't joke as much, smile real stiff, can stare you down til you feel like a pile of salt waiting to blow away with the breeze. And I guess I just don't want you to be that way. I'm scared you not gonna be the same man I knew before. I really want to see the paper you wrote. That's all. I just wanted you to share it with me too. So why don't you get it back from Ms. Harris and let me see it too, okay?

Love,

Natasha

August 4, 1990
Natasha,

Well, here it is. I hope you like it. It's probably not good as what you could do, but Ms. Harris liked it enough to get me in the GED class that's gonna start in the fall. And she ain't the only one trying to school me. Mohammed saw me reading Catcher in the Rye *and asked me why I was reading shit that didn't have nothing to do with me. I told him I had read it in school and my teacher took the time to bring me my book and I was gonna read it and appreciate it just like the books he had. So he gave me one of his books from the milk crates he got all over our room. I heard of it before.* Autobiography of Malcolm X. *I told him I wasn't stupid and I knew about Malcolm X from learning about him in Black History Month and going on that damn walking tour with Mr. Cook where he showed us places where he lived, and from movies on TV. I thought him and Benito was gonna get into it when Benito said Don't be corruptin the youngun with your angry black man bullshit that ain't got you nowhere but in the pen. Mohammed told Benito to shut up and read the dictionary so he could learn English. Then he told me I got a new teacher in town, and it was about time I started reading something that was relevent before it was too late. He was telling me that Malcolm X was uneducated before he went in, but he came out a genius cause he read the dictionary back and forth a thousand times. Now, I ain't doing nothing like that. I might do it once, but that's it. So between Ms. Harris and Mohammed I'm gonna come out here a professor and shit. Lawyer already told me I'm supposed to be a genius. It might be some truth to that shit. Mohammed found a Rubik's Cube in one of his crates. I ain't seen one of them things for years. It was all fucked up and he said he had been trying to get it back to normal for years. I did it in two days. My partners on the block started coming down here fucking that shit up all crazy, I mean turning that thing for two and three hours trying to get it to the point that I couldn't solve it again. Every time they fucked it up, I put it right back together again. Inmates and guards from other blocks heard about that shit and started coming down trying to catch me up. It's like a battle almost. Mohammed call it a "meeting of the minds." You know he gotta say some intellectual shit, but yo this is fun. I get to see things all fucked up and coming back together again and plan five, six, seven steps ahead. I wish I could have done that on the outside, with my life.*

Love,
Antonio

Holden and Me: What I think about the book
The Catcher in the Rye
By Michael Antonio Lawrence II

The first time I read The Catcher in the Rye *I got* mad at my teacher, Mr. Cook, for giving us something that at first seems like it's about nothing. For one

thing, the main character is a boy named Holden Caulfield who seem like he have it all. He go to this fancy school named Pencey in upstate New York when the only time most cats I know go upstate is for this, the pen. At this school he got a dorm room and they eat stuff like steak for dinner every Saturday when most people I know only have steak on their birthday. Well he basically get kicked out of school and go back to New York where he from—the fancy part of Manhattan maybe—and instead of going home he choose to explore the city and hook up with old girlfriends and prostitutes and other people of that nature. It seem to me that all this white boy did was complain complain complain—about his friends, the teachers, the food, his parents, girls—or babes is what they used to say back then. The way he looked at everything was negative. He had a chance at something most kids would kill for. A chance to live away from home and go somewhere different and be on your own and get an allowance. But he chose to focus on the negative instead and by page fifty I was through with him. Also the fact that he was always lonely or depressed or crying and not knowing why, like he was a bottle of soda ready to explode with all this emotion but nobody had even shook the bottle. But something kept me reading this book. I think it was the fact that Holden was lonely, that deep down inside he felt like nobody was understanding who he was or that he wasn't making a real connection with anybody. It's one part in the book when he says that New York is a terrible place when somebody laughs on the street late at night and when you hear that laugh you get so sad because it makes you feel so lonely and depressed. I remember thinking when I first read that how could somebody get lonely in a place like NYC where everywhere you look its people people everywhere? People behind you on line, people in front of you making you late, people hogging up the seats on the train, people bumping into you while they on the go and not even saying I'm sorry. I had to come here to figure out what he really meant by that. Because I find myself surrounded every day all day by grown men, angry men older than me with wrinkles and scars and yellow eyes to tell you where they been. And I don't want to get sucked up into that lonely, a part of that place that feels like a sewer filled with dreams flushed away. So I stopped hating Holden and starting feeling for him when I saw him floating around our city, with no place to really call home and no friends to help ease the ride. One thing that help him through is thinking about his sister Phoebe, cause even though she only nine, Holden knows that she understands him and got his back no matter what. That's how I feel about my moms and my girl, like if I was halfway across the world with no place to lay my head and rest that there is someone that would always welcome me home with open arms. Whenever I think about them, I get like Holden and start bawl-

*ing as he put it. I'm gonna be like Holden and say I
don't know why that is. It just is.*

■

August 10, 1990
Antonio,

Antonio, I really love your essay. You wrote that all by
yourself? I don't believe it. See, I knew you could do a lot
better in school than you was doing. And baby, don't
worry, you will never be like those other dudes in there
with you cause I won't ever let you get that hopeless. You
gonna be just like Holden when you get out, able to
walk around and go anywhere you want and explore the
whole city. Only the difference is you gonna have somebody waiting for you soon as you get out. That somebody is me! You never told me that you cry when you
think about me. I cry when I think about you too because I miss you, but hopefully, that will all be over soon.

Antonio, you've asked me to keep a lot of secrets, so
now I have to ask you to keep one. You can't tell nobody
this, not Black, not even your mother, cause right now
we don't know what we gonna do. But Laneice is pregnant. She had told me last week that she skipped her period, and Laneice got her period when she was only nine
and she ain't never skipped it in almost 8 years so she
said she knew something was up. So, we went to the
store to get that EPT test, and we did it here while Roy

and my mother was at work. And it came out positive. You know, that little pink line had appeared. She started crying and breathing real hard and shaking real bad and I had to just tell her to get it together, that this wasn't the time for her to lose control.

We gonna go to that adolescent clinic that's on 96th Street on the East Side just to make sure, and then see what we could do about it. But she said she don't want nobody to know cause she don't want it getting back to Black just in case she wanna get an abortion. I told that girl this was gonna happen if she wasn't careful. Don't you remember I told you that I had warned her? She told me to not even tell you, so Antonio I'm trusting you with this information. Don't even tell none of your friends in jail cause you never know who knows who, and it could get back to whoever. She ain't telling her big brother or her little sister. She said she don't wanna tell her little sister cause she feel like she gotta set an example for her, and if her big sis get knocked up, then she might think it's okay to get knocked up too. And she said her big brother might come up from Rutgers and kill Black. Plus Laneice real scared cause you know her mother and father don't play that. I mean, they give that girl everything. They live in that nice brownstone and Laneice got that big room all to herself. She got all the fresh gear and Mrs. Clark pay for her to get her hair done every week. They all go to church together every Sunday, and then they go out to lunch or brunch or something like that so they can have the family outings like her mother say. I done been out with them myself, and her parents seem real cool. Always telling her to sit up straight and keep her elbows off the table and act like a lady. Well, they won't be too happy if they find out little Miss Perfect bout to be a single mother. They gonna be real mad, they probably gonna kill her. Mrs. Clark one of them uppity black ladies, wear the white gloves and shit. They might force her to get an abortion or send her far away from Harlem and she said she can't stand to be away from Black. Well, I don't know what she gonna do. She ain't got no money. Laneice ain't never had to work, so she don't have money saved up like I do. And Black ain't got NO MONEY. Matter fact he owe me ten dollars now cause I fronted his way to the movies so many times. I told Laneice that if she really really needed an abortion, that I would give her the money. I mean, she my girl. We been friends for a real long time, since we was in second grade. I got about 500 dollars saved up, the money I was gonna use for France, but I told her I would let her have it and she could pay me back if she really needed it. We would have to figure out how to get to Jersey though, where we could do it without NOBODY finding out. I mean, this is serious. Well, I'm gonna let you know what happens. What we figure out. But remember. Don't tell nobody.

Love,
Natasha

August 14, 1990
Natasha

First of all, I ain't got no friends in here. Just cause I see these cats every day and eat with em and shower with em don't make em my friends. That's the first thing Mookie and MGD told me. If you get sent up, you ain't got no friends in there. Your life is on the outside and you just deal with who you gotta deal with in the joint, maintain til you can get back to it. Don't trust nobody. Don't confide in nobody. Folks always looking for information from the streets and they'll use you to get it. Keep shit to yourself. And watch your ass, and they mean really watch your ass. So you ain't gotta worry about me talking to nobody. Far as I'm concerned, I don't need to associate with nobody but Mohammed and Benito, and that's just cause I see them every day. And I think they really do like me. They cool. Really don't bother me that much, I go my way they go theirs. We don't hang out together in the yard or nothin, we just kinda nod and smile at each other. I mean, I know if something was to happen to me, that they would have my back. Same way I would have theirs. That go without saying. It's just kind of an unspoken rule that we have between us.

Well, this might come as a surprise to you, but I already knew about Laneice. Black told me. He wrote me this big old note said MAN I'M BOUT TO HAVE A SHORTY REAL SOON!!!!! So it's some things your girl ain't telling you. She done already told her man and they mak-

ing plans and shit about living together. So she pulling your leg with this abortion shit. You might wanna check her on it. Just FYI, CYA like Mohammed always been saying. Write me back soon, baby girl. I gotta go now cause Ms. Harris hooked me up to maybe get a job a lot earlier than I'm eligible. So I got a interview and shit to work with Housekeeping. Just cleaning up and mopping shit, but least I can get out of this room sometime. Oh, and that peach fuzz you used to love to kiss is turning into a real goatee. Pretty soon I won't look like the youngun. When you come out here soon, you'll see. I'm gonna look like a real man.

Love,
Antonio

■

August 16, 1990

Antonio, can you believe what Laneice did to me and we supposed to be friends? Can you believe what she would do to me and we been friends now for almost ten years? She lied to me Antonio. She told me that she needed to get an abortion but she couldn't ask her parents for the money, of course. So, me being the nice person that I am and the good friend that I am, I told her that I would loan her the money. Now, all I got in the bank from working at Macy's is about $500, and I told her that was my money for France but that I would give it to her

cause she was my girl and I know she would do the same
for me. Well, come to find out, this bitch used my money
not for an abortion but to run away from home. Her
mother came over our house at 3:00 in the morning crying and screaming and wondering where Laneice was. I
didn't have no idea. I had just talked to the girl that
morning. So Mr. and Mrs. Clark and my mother and me
was driving around Harlem and the Bronx looking for
her. Funny thing was, Black wasn't at home either but
his parents used to him disappearing when he wanna. I
mean, boys can get away with anything. That's just the
way it is.

But the next day, Laneice come calling me whispering
and shit from a pay phone, talking about her and Black
was in Baltimore and they had took the bus down there
and they was about to stay with some of his cousins and
find a job. Now they ain't had no money so guess where
they got the money for the bus tickets and food and
stuff? You guessed it—me! I was like, "No y'all ain't
bitch! Not with my money." She said, "Natasha, please
don't be mad at me I'm gonna pay it back but I wanna
keep my baby and I didn't want my mother to kill me."
Can you believe her? Can you believe Black? They supposed to be my homies, I mean both of them almost like
my own fam and I trusted them with my loot and this is
what they do? I'm through with her Antonio. I mean
that. We are NOT friends anymore. She supposed to be
coming back, cause her mother and father gonna drive
down MD and get her. But when she get back, we not

gonna be girlz no more Antonio and I mean that. I'm leaving for France on Saturday and I ain't got NO MONEY cause I felt sorry for her. Now, my money is spent and that bitch is still pregnant, so they ain't did shit but waste my money on some hot dogs and chips and soda and bus tickets. And she not even staying down there so NOTHING is resolved. And this how she repay a true friend? Well, fuck her. With friends like that, I can roll by myself. I got Tamika and Valencia to be my girlz if she don't want the job. Matter of fact the program took us to the Hall of Science in Queens and we all took this picture together that I put in a frame that says "Friends Forever." So Laneice better just get ready to pick a new godmother for her baby cause it ain't gonna be me. Not after this. We're finished. I told my mother about what she did. Mommy went into the vase that she keep on top of the armoire in her room, where Roy just see incense sticking out and don't know nothing in the bottom. She gave me all the money that was in there for my trip, about seventy dollars and even five Susan B. Anthony dollars she said she had been holding on to cause she was hoping they would be worth something one day. Write me back soon, and tell Black when you write him that I'm through with his woman!

Love,
Natasha

August 20, 1990

Well Natasha, I know you in France right now, that you flew above the world and looked down on it. Did you imagine you could see me? Did you believe that I was looking up at you at the same time you was looking down? I know you made it safe cause I called your mother house to find out if you had called. She told me Natasha so happy she was talking a mile a minute and I couldn't understand a word she was saying and then she just got up off the phone cause she said her phone card was running out. I actually kicked it with your mom for a few minutes. I didn't even think she would accept the charges, but she did and she even talked to me for a while. She told me the ring I gave you was pretty, and she asked me how I was doing in there and did I miss home and good food and stuff. She said that the next time you came to visit, she was gonna send me a plate—some ribs and mac and cheese and my favorite banana pudding if she could freeze it for me. Then she had to jump, but I was glad I had a chance to talk to your moms for a minute.

But to tell you the truth, Natasha, I'm a little bit upset thinking about you so far away from me. It's different when I know you at home, when I can picture you in your room sitting on the bed with all those teddy bears around you, in your blue pajamas with the curvy moons on them. But I can't imagine you anywhere but Harlem. I can't picture Paris, don't know what it look like and how you look in it. For the first time since all this shit started, I feel like you could slip away from me. Like you could get so far away from me, not just your body, but your heart and your mind, and I could be all alone again. I know you think I'm not alone now but really I am even though it's people around me all the time. I'm alone because it's nobody around who truly understands me and who I am on the inside, what I look like when I'm just myself and ain't putting on no airs cause I don't have to be tough or something I'm not.

See, in here, I'm #007624, the young nigger who would snuff his own daddy so he don't give a fuck about snuffing you. That's cool cause that mean I gets my respect and nobody bother me, but that's not who I am. You know the real me. The real me who like to chase down Mister Softee for those cherry bombs, the real me who like impersonating characters off TV, the real me who still wear baby lotion cause I like the way it smell. You know me and you know all that. I mean, Trevon and Black know me too and I can let my guard down around them, but I still can't get all soft with them. So it's hard for me to think about you so far away, meeting new people and different guys and stuff that might make you forget about the real me and focus on the me that fucked up and got put in here. But I hope you having fun in France, getting to see that Mona Lisa painting and shit. I wouldn't mind seeing all that myself. Maybe when I get out you can teach me some French and me and you can go to Paris together. What do you think?

Love,
Antonio

August 21, 1990

Bonjour Bonjour Monsieur,

Antonio, do you see this big building on the front of this card? It's call The Eiffel Tower and me, Valencia, and Tamika standing right in front of it right now and it really is as tall as what it looks like. Just like the Empire State Building and the Statue of Liberty. See New York ain't the only spot with buildings so tall you feel like you can touch the sky. I miss you and I'm having so much fun and I will tell you all about it when I get back.

Au revoir,

Natasha

PS. You know that real famous picture called the Mona Lisa where the lady is sitting smiling real funny? Well, I saw that picture yesterday can you believe it!?!

August 25, 1990

Natasha baby, I can't write much and I don't even know if you gonna be able to see this letter but hopefully you will. The whole place here is on lockdown. We have to eat in our rooms, we have to go to the showers five at a time, no gym, no yard, no basketball, no rec. I was supposed to start my GED classes today but when I asked about it the c.o. just hissed at me and told me to shut the fuck up. So I just sit quiet and wait for a guard to call my name: #007624.

There was a fight yesterday, between these two cats who had beef dating back three years or something like that, when they was on the outside and they brought it here. I don't know em, but they call one Fat Albert cause he look like the cartoon and the other one just named Joe. But that's not why we on lockdown. When they started fighting, the cracker guards took it too far and got out of control. It took five of them to hold down Fat Albert but they didn't stop there. By the time they got finished, niggaz was slipping on his blood and a few guards faces was red as blood from the chokeholds they had em in. Then everybody else got delirious and started banging they trays on the table and one crazy white boy with pimples all over his face—we call him Tiny—started screaming so loud it made my eardrums vibrate. Spit was coming down from his mouth and he was saying over and over and over again Lets do this and be out, let's do this and be out. It took twenty minutes to get enough guards to control everybody. They beat em down and dragged them away. Fat Albert in the infirm and I heard he ain't gonna make it.

But I knew it was coming, I knew something was going to give. Yesterday I felt something in the air, something was teasing the back of my neck like static electricity, I felt the sad in the air like you can smell rain before it fall. Benito been whispering that woman's name and I finally figured out it's Gloria. Mohammed been silent leaning against the

wall all day, with his eyes closed and his mouth moving.
Today the sun passed by our tiny window.
    Love,
    Antonio

■

August 26, 1990
Antonio,

I'm sorry I can't write much, but I just got back and I'm
writing this now while I'm on the A train coming from
Kennedy. I have to tell you something, sweetheart, and
you have to promise not to get mad at me. I'm not gonna
drag it out, I'm just gonna go ahead and say it. I lost the
ring, baby. I think I lost some weight from working so
much, and maybe my finger shrunk or something cause
we was walking down this long bridge to look at this
river called the Seine and I leaned over to take a picture
and the ring just slipped off and fell in the water. And I
swear to God I wanted to jump in and find it, but then I
remembered I couldn't swim and we was about twenty
feet in the air. Antonio, I cried and cried all day and I
didn't have no fun the rest of the trip. I got a long ways
to go before I get uptown, but I'm supposed to write an
essay totally in French about my trip and what I learned.
Which I promise I'm going to tell you all about it—the
food, the TV channels with naked people on them in the
daytime, all the Africans over there that look like mod-

els. But all in all Paris looked a little like New York, but a lot cleaner with a lot more churches. I mean, you had the people everywhere packed in so tight on the sidewalks we could barely move. There was a street called the Champs Elysées with shops and stores just like 5th Ave. There was this place called the Latin Quarter that looked kind of like the Village with all these little shops in the basement and people drinking coffee and wine at tables outside. I saw people of all different races and everybody spoke English. We couldn't even practice our French because everybody knew we were American and wanted to practice English with us. It was so pretty over there, Antonio. The statues and sculpture and painting everywhere. Even the buildings looked like art because pictures were painted on the sides. Not dirty graffiti pictures but art that looked like it belonged in the museum. I was walking around the whole time like I was in outer space, with my mouth open and my eyes all wide. I know they could tell I was a tourist! Remember when we would go to Times Square and play "trip the tourist"? Well, I know I should have been tripped a few times cause I was soaking up everything and staring like I didn't know what a big city was. It was way better than New York, Antonio. A lot better. I didn't even want to come back. I wanted to stay at least another week, but I guess all good things have to come to an end.

But I need to take a little nap while I'm on this train. I've already missed a few days of school so I'm gonna to have to make that up, plus Mommy say Laneice been calling me cause she wanna talk and I decided I'm gonna go ahead and be her girl again. Least til she have the baby cause she gonna need somebody, cause her parents don't support her at all. But I'm gonna try to come and see you the next time your mother take the bus up there. It's been too long since we saw each other and maybe my punishment for that was losing the ring. Antonio, I'm trying not to say that I really lost it because it's floating out there in the world, a sign that no matter where we are our love is forever. My grandmother used to take me and Drew to Riverside Park so we could watch the Hudson. She told us that rivers connect everybody in the whole world to one God like veins in the body that pump blood from one heart. So maybe now that my ring is somewhere out there in the world, it means we're even more connected than before. I'm sorry I lost your ring, but I'll get another one and buy you one too. I promise that on all I love.

Natasha

PART THREE

October 11, 1990
Dear Natasha,

I know it's only been about two weeks since the last time you wrote me, but in here, two weeks seem like two years. Time means nothing cause contrary to popular belief things don't get better with time in here, but time means everything cause when it's finally over things will all be better. Sometimes I feel like the only thing I have to do is wait for you, like a kid waiting for Christmas or a dead tree waiting on spring. I count the days til I see your smile again, til I can poke my middle finger in that dimple on your left cheek and make you laugh, when I can see what kind of hairstyle you rocking or what color you painted your toes. Work is cool although it's boring as Sunday school. Well, maybe not as boring as Sunday school cause that shit is pretty damn boring. Few times my mother did make me go, I fell asleep and was snoring and slobbing till she slapped me awake. But it's just a little bit repetitive cause I'm responsible for the same wing. It ain't hard really, just mopping up the floors and wiping down the showers. Not as nasty as I thought it would be cause we always do a pretty good job of keeping things up. I got my books. I finished the Malcolm X book and now Mohammed got me reading Soul on Ice *by this man named Eldridge Cleaver. Ms. Harris like my*

Catcher in the Rye *paper so she gave me a bunch of other books she thought I might like,* The Outsiders *which I was supposed to read for Mr. Cook and this book called* The Jungle *about these poor warehouse workers in slaughterhouses and shit.*

Thank you for all the Fresh *mags you been sending me. Benito made me put Janet and Lisa Lisa and Salt on my wall (Benito got* Pepa *cause he like her thighs). But anyway I got my classes, which is going pretty good. I'm learning about all that shit I never bothered to pay attention to in school, like the Boston Tea Party and the Constitution and whatever. I wanna get my GED by January so I can start some correspondence courses and get a college degree. Ms. Harris really like me a lot, bringing me all these pamphlets and shit from different schools cross the country. What you think about me being a veterinarian? You think I could do that baby? It would be long and hard, but I think I could do it. I ain't told nobody I was thinking about it but you and Ms. Harris. Well, Benito's crazy ass, but what he know?*

I told him, Benito I like science. I was always feeling it in school but I wasn't trying to be a nerd or no shit like that. Benito was like, What you know about working with animals? I told him I live with you, don't I? Benito one of them cats ain't got no problems laughing at himself, so he thought that shit was funny. But I told him I don't know shit, but that was the point of going to school, to learn. He said some shit like You ain't just gonna be dealing with dogs and cats you gonna have to deal with everything—

snakes, horses . . . I saw on the animal planet where they had to give a elephant at the Bronx Zoo an enema. I thought that shit was so funny. I couldn't stop laughing. I laughed until tears came down from my eyes and my stomach was hurting and I started choking on the flaming hot Cheetos you know I eat every day. Can you imagine me giving a elephant an enema? A grown man sticking his hands up in an elephant's ass? I asked Benito that question and he said that he had already seen it, the other day in the showers before he left to give the perpetrators some privacy. I swear, Benito is one cool Rican. It feels good to have somebody to make me laugh.

I miss laughing as much as I used to. I miss hearing rain fall on the fire escape. I miss my aunt's sweet potato pie and half-n-halfs at Manna's. I miss sipping brew on the stoop with my daddy and the other old cats I used to look up to. I miss hearing the Mister Softee truck and basketballs bouncing on real cement. I miss wilding out in the Jackie Robinson pool, dunking you and scaring you cause you can't swim and trying to kiss your breasts under the water. I miss seeing my mother's face. I miss you.

Love,
Antonio

■

October 20, 1990
Dear Antonio,

You're right that it seem like more and more time does pass now between our letters, but the truth is, baby, time is tight for me right now. I got back to Harlem and things been moving full speed ahead since then. The block, the apartment, school, everything looks so much smaller than it did before I left. It don't even take me that long to walk down 125th Street anymore, and I used to think that was the longest street in the world. Laneice been stressing me out with all this baby shit. She done went from talking bout Black all the time to talking about shorties and shopping for shorties and I don't want to hear it cause I'm trying to maintain and I got problems of my own. This SAT class is kicking my ass and I might have to cut my hours back, which mean I'm gonna have less cheddar. Mommy's really serious about this house thing and she been trying to get her shit together. I went downtown with her twice to talk to people at banks and we even went to HUD. Remember Housing and Urban Development that we learned about in school?

I haven't been out of Harlem with Ma in a very long time, and it was nice. We walked around a little bit downtown on Canal Street where she bought me some earrings and a new LV bag, from the vendors. We held hands cause of all the people pushing and shoving past each other trying to get from point A to point B. She getting excited about everything. She told me she gonna make us a family again. She told me, "Natasha, I gave birth to both my kids, not just one, so it ain't right for my only son not to be under my roof, for me not to be seeing his face every morning and kissing him at night." I told her, "Mommy don't worry. Everything gonna be alright. Me and you gonna do this together. I'm gonna help you with all the paperwork and all the forms and looking for the furniture. We can go up to 125th and get those pretty African sculptures and those paintings of stuff like black men holding their kids and black women with them real colorful wraps on their head." She just laughed at me when we had finally walked down all of Canal, almost to the Manhattan Bridge going to Brooklyn. She was like, "You make it all sound so easy." I snapped my fingers and told her, "It is easy. Let's just do this and be out!" She told me, "Kids always think everything is so easy, but it's a lot you all never know." I wanted to tell her, "Mommy, I ain't no kid no more. I ain't got a daddy or a big brother to fight my battles—I gotta fight them myself. I got a job, I done traveled around the world all by myself with no one to help me, I'm going to college soon, and most important I got a man locked up and that'll make a woman outta any girl." But I knew she wouldn't understand all that. She don't see I had to grow up fast too, the way she always tell me she had to grow up. I knew she would just laugh and think I was still the same little Natasha blowing bubbles off the fire escape and almost falling to the street trying to catch em.

But I say all this, Antonio, to say that I guess I just don't have the time I used to have. It's not the summertime no more, I can't spend my whole day writing letters. It's just not possible, specially with this program making me come to City College every Tuesday and Thursday night for this SAT class for college. I gotta take the test soon so I can apply to college by January and February which is when most of the deadlines are. So I'm just handling my business the same way you handling yours, it's just that I don't have all the time you have, with school and work and everything. Long as I keep handling my biz, I can keep my mind off you and thinking about everything you must be going through. I miss you too baby, and I'm just trying to keep it together til we can be together again. I'm riding up there with your ma in two weeks. Laneice and Black wanna come with us. She swelling already believe it or not, and it's only been three months. They say they want me and you to be the godmother and godfather. What you think about that baby? Being godparents until we get our own?

Love your baby mama (future),

Natasha

October 22, 1990
Dear Ms. Harris,

The reason I didn't show up for my tutoring today was cause I was feeling too down to face the world. I went to work, mess hall, showers. Work is a bitch cause it's freezing in the work room and they won't give us no heat. Just did the shit I had to do cause I had to do it. I know I got to keep up with my classes, but that's the one thing these moth- erfuckers don't care if I do or not.

Last night I had a dream I was back on the outside and my mother gave me a party at the house. I could smell food but I couldn't see it—fried chicken mostly, some apple pie and biscuits and my favorite banana pudding. It was one of them big WELCOME HOME signs hanging from wall to wall in the living room and it said BY TYLER AND TREVON at the bottom. And everybody in the whole world who I know by name was there—you, my girl, peo- ple from school, my lawyer, the detectives that came to pick me up, the warden, my teacher Mr. Cook, them guys MGD and Mookie I had told you about, Benito, Mohammed, my brothers and aunts and cousins and neighbors. I mean, not they whole body cause we only got two bedrooms and a tiny kitchen and it's only so much that can fit. But it was like they was there and I felt them and I saw everybody's face floating in the air, so thin and shadowlike that I could put my hand through it, poke my fingers through their eyes and mouth without them frowning or squinting. My body felt weak and loose, like while I was walking parts of me was falling off, hitting the ground without a sound. I didn't care about picking them up and saving them for later so a doctor could put em back on.

There was only one person who was there and whole in the flesh. It was my daddy, sitting on the couch with the remote in one hand and a bottle of vodka in the other. He had on this checkered robe me and my brothers bought him up at Harlem Mart for Father's Day. I think he was naked up under it cause it was open so I could see far up his thighs and his stomach rolling soft and yellow like a little puppy's belly. And he looked at me and smiled, and said, Tony you want me to cook you some eggs? You want some eggs? And I smiled cause Daddy ain't called me Tony since I was a little boy. And I said while I heard all the people in the world talking and laughing and singing old songs I knew, Yeah Daddy that sound good. And he put down his drink and tied up his robe and got up and pat my shoulder real quick and soft when he passed me and said Okay Tony I'll fix you some eggs.

November 7, 1990
Dear Antonio:

I'm so sorry it has taken me so long to respond to your letter. I don't know if I had told you that I was getting married, but I had my wedding on October 28 and I have been on my honeymoon. My husband and I have been in Trinidad where he's originally from. We were visiting his parents and we just returned Sunday. I had a beautiful time and can tell you all about this wonderful country when I next see you. It's definitely a place that I would recommend you visit in your lifetime. But back to your letter. Antonio, please don't beat yourself up about missing class. As a matter of fact, the tutors told me that you have not shown up for the last three classes. Antonio, you were doing really well and I know that with your natural intelligence and some disciplined studying, you could have your GED by the end of the winter. Then, we could move on to a new challenge for you. I know that you may be feeling hopeless about your situation, frightened about the repercussions of what you have done. I imagine that you have an enormous amount of guilt chipping away at your soul. It is okay and very natural for you to have these feelings. I wish that more resources were available to help you deal with your unique situation. It still amazes me how little counseling inmates receive in the American justice system, given that rehabilitation is supposed to be the point of incarceration. However, giving up on yourself is not the answer. Lying in your room all day staring at the ceiling is not how to face your fears. This is the time when you must reach deep inside yourself, pull out everything you have and know in order to push ahead and finish what you have started. There are a lot of people who believe in you—me, your fiancée, your mother, your little brothers, your former teachers. You

just have to believe in yourself. Please come back to tutoring as soon as you feel up to it.

Sincerely,

Ms. Harris

PS. Maybe it would help if you wrote your father a letter.
Write to him just as you write to me, your mother, your
fiancée. Tell him how you feel. Read it or rip it up when
you finish. JUST WRITE!

*21 21 21 21 times 21 21 21 member that time you made
me eat trevon's shit cause the toilet wasn't working and they
wouldn't come fix it even though you had called twenty-one
times you kept saying twenty one times twenty one goddamn
times and you got mad cause I flushed it but I didn't know it
was broke so it overflowed and it stayed broke even though
you called them twenty one more times to come and fix it
member that time you wrapped the coconut for my birthday
cake in a pillowcase and beat trevon naked naked and
skinny and little and shaking but he wouldn't cry that little
nigger had heart he wouldn't cry you hit him where nobody
would see right in his nuts I saw you aiming for his nuts
cause he let it slip to the principal where the bruises came
from member that time you slit my mommy's face with the razor that she shaved you with almost every night and remember how her face hung down away from her bones like meat
in the butcher shop and you laughed motherfucker you
laughed while she bled and I watched I watched we watched*

while she cried and you kicked her and you waved your razor at us like it was a sword and I remember I was only 11 and I had just read White Fang in my room and I wanted the fighting the noise the yelling the fighting the noise to stop so I came out to tell you all about it to tell you that your seed wasn't stupid your seed can read so be happy and stop fighting cause Antonio Michael Lawrence the II can read but when I came out you was beating her so I thought the edges of the blade looked like teeth a wolf's teeth waiting to rush me and eat out my heart so I stood there I stood there I couldn't speak I couldn't talk I didn't even call 911 I stood there and waited for you to stop laughing and I wanted you to start loving us and her and be happy to come home not mad not tired not sweaty not smelling like garbage not mumbling but really looking me in the eye and talking to me like I was your son but all you ever gave me was your back all you ever gave her was your hand all you ever gave us was commands you told me what not to do in life but you never told me what to do you never told me to love to read to dance to play ball to reproduce to keep my back arched and my fingers closed when I swim to hold my hands far apart on the bat to keep my balance on the bike to hold my pencil right to shave up not down to wear a rubber when I fucked to tell the girl I was diggin that I was really diggin her why was you so mad why couldn't you just tell me why you was mad I was ashamed I was scared I didn't want nobody to know I hated you and now that I'm here I don't give no fuck I don't give no fuck who read my shit or who know I planned what I did cause I'm in here now I'm here regardless ten years I'm here for

*what I did so I might as well just go ahead and tell you pop
I planned it from the beginning I even got it written down in
a notebook Mr. Cook gave me with the big X for Malcolm X
on the front it say if my daddy ever get ready to touch me or
my brothers or my mother again I'm gonna go get the piece
that Black showed me his cousin got in the closet and I'm going to cock back that safety and I'm gonna shoot that son of
a bitch I'm going to aim it right in the middle of his head
and make you look me in the eye for the first time cause you
never did it on your own I wanna make you look me in the
eye for the first and last time before I make you disappear and
die it wasn't even cold that night I did it so when I walked
to Black's spot to get the piece it wasn't even cold no coat no
hat no gloves no scarf my mommy's screams playing over and
over and over again in my head kept me warm and I came
back and I did what I said I was gonna do cause I'm a man
and you told me don't ever go back on your word and I didn't
go back on my word I did it and I didn't even need a piece all
I had to do was reach in the sink imagine that all that time
I could have done it all that time and it wasn't even cold and
it wasn't even hard and it wasn't even scary and I didn't
even miss you that much until now*

November 15, 1990

Antonio, that Ms. Harris lady done called our house and
your mother's house basically saying you up there going

crazy. All you do is lay in your bed all day staring at Benito's mattress. She said you lost your job cause you ain't been showing up. Basically what happened was I was in the kitchen frying salmon cakes and boiling peas and rice cause Grandma and Drew was coming over for dinner. This blocked number came up on the caller ID and Roy told me to get it just in case it was a bill collector so I could talk my 10 year old voice and say nobody was there. Well, I was about to hang up soon as I answered cause she sounded like a white woman and the only time they call is when we past due on bills or I been skipping school. So I just said real quick, "We ain't here and if we was, we ain't interested." And she said, "No, wait. My name is Dream Harris and I'm the educational counselor for Michael Lawrence." So I said, "Yeah yeah yeah, he done talked about you." She sounded like a real nice lady, just white-talking like Laneice mother. And that's when she proceeded to tell me all about what you been doing, or haven't been doing I should say. She was like, "I'm very concerned about Michael and I really don't know what to do to get him back into the swing of things." She said she was hoping I could talk to you, give you "a jolt" she called it. She said that she had already talked to your moms, but that she didn't seem like she was listening. I didn't want her to think bad about your mother, cause I swear I love her like my own, so I told her "Mrs. Lawrence good peoples she just kind of depressed that's all." She sent me a copy of the letter she wrote you. She said you hadn't wrote her back yet and that wasn't like you. But I promised this woman I would talk to you, try to convince you to come back.

I'm on the number 3 bus right now, going down Manhattan Avenue bout to pass 123rd, and let me tell you what I see. The sky is blue. The leaves on the trees are sherbert colors: orange, peach, and yellow. I can see our house, Douglass Gardens, down the street and they finished putting the pretty red bricks on the outside and now they fixing up the inside. I can see the shiny white spiral staircase down the middle, and the chandelier hanging down like the sun. I can see our porch with pretty decorated handles on the side, with steps all our own and not no nasty stoop that belong to the whole building where people can piss and hang out. Our steps are gonna have flowers on em and be clean enough so I can sit out with my girlz and my moms and watch Harlem go by. I can see the white door with a glass window that have pretty frosted designs on it. I can see me and you behind that door, eating at a big old dining room table with a really bright, expensive painting hanging on the wall right above a bookcase with all our books. I can see all of that. Open your eyes and you can see it too.

Love,
Natasha

November 20, 1990
Hey Baby Girl,

So Ms. Harris care that much about me that she calling my house and shit to talk about me? I feel really bad now that I been missing class, but to tell you the truth Natasha, I just don't feel like doing shit. It's so hard for me to move my body and I feel weak all the time. I'm gonna keep this letter short cause my hands is shaking and my eyes ain't focusing too good. You don't know what this is like. You don't know how it is to live your life in a place where everything is hard—the beds, the floors, the stares from people all around you, the bodies piled up on top of each other. I took a lot of shit for granted when I didn't know any better. The softness of leaves, grass. The luxury of falling asleep on the living room couch with the TV on until the static wakes you up. The feeling of rain on my face and your tongue in my mouth. I stare out of this tiny window sometimes and all I can think is, God, I never knew the sky was that blue. On the outside, the sky was just another thing in my world that I didn't take the time to notice, like the people who really cared about me, the food that was always on the stove when I got home, the Christmas presents that showed up even though Ma and Daddy didn't do shit but say they had no money. Now, I find myself walking in the yard or looking out of the window sometimes and I can't take my eyes off the sky, like it's the last thing on earth I'll ever see.

I wasn't feeling this way a few weeks ago, before Mo-hammed stopped talking to everybody cause his parole got denied. Now my corner of the world got a damper over it. Benito been trying to make jokes to crack us up, but I can tell you it's not working.

I got even more down too when my peoples came to visit me. When I was looking out at you and Laneice and Black and my brothers, I saw the same kids from off the block haven't changed a bit. Still young, still fresh with them shiny eyes and bright faces, still green like they say in The Outsiders. *And just a little bit I could see the reflection of my own face in the glass, thin and see-through like the shadow faces I keep seeing in my dreams. And all I could think while looking at you all at the same time I was look-ing at me was I look old, I look sad, I look used. Seeing people you care about is supposed to get your spirits up, keep your mental up and focused on the finish line. But it had the opposite effect on me. It got me down and reminded me of all I'm missing out on. So I don't think I want you all to come see me anymore. I'll have to think about that, but I'm pretty sure that's the way I want it. I'm pretty sure that's the way it has to be.*

Love,
#007624

November 28, 1990
Dear Antonio,

I can tell something wrong with you cause of the way your letter look, all sloppy and little and words running damn near off the page. I can't take worrying about you now. I can't take no more on my head than I already got. I can't worry about nobody else. I gotta be the only one worry about Mommy now cause Grandma's gone, Antonio. Grandma died on Wednesday in church. We at her house right now with people bringing food and stuff. Everybody downstairs—Laneice came, Valencia and Tamika came too. But I need to be alone. I'm laying in her and Grandpa old bed so I don't have to be around nobody.

We just had a wake at the church. It was a nice little service. Grandma was almost 75 years old and she barely got one line in her face, her hair just as black and straight as if she had just got it pressed. A lot of singing and people getting up saying things about Grandma. I didn't know she had so many friends, but I guess old people like to keep a tight crew too. It was fine up until the end when we had to go look at the body. Drew wouldn't stop crying and he wouldn't take his hands off Grandma pretty pink dress so they could close the casket and Mommy and Roy had to pull him off. He got so mad about that he pushed Roy and said, "You ain't my daddy," and then the mortician shut the casket real quick, just when I was putting my hand in it. He gave me this real mean look with his eyes and closed it before I could see Grandma face and touch her and say goodbye. That uppity Negro fucked up the last time I could ever see my grandma. She probably cremated by now, cause that's what she wanted. The preacher man from her church say Grandma went the way she was supposed to go, serving God cause that's what she loved most next to her family. The holy ladies who brought Drew home and been bringing food over say she got the holy ghost and started running around the pews with her hands in the air and her body shouting and nobody knew nothing was wrong. So rather than helping her they just encouraged her on, singing and clapping and jingling their tambourines louder. Then she let out one big last shout they say and just fell in front of the preacher with her hands on her heart and tears in her eyes.

Mommy fainted when they told her and we had to put her in the tub with ice cubes before she would wake up. Then she just started moaning real loud saying, "Who I got now? Who I got to take care of me?" And the holy ladies told her, "You got Jesus and you got yourself honey and you got your kids now to take care of you." And all I was thinking was, what about me? Who's gonna worry about me? I have to take that damn SAT test next weekend and I'm gonna fail cause I have too much on my mind. Then I'm not gonna go to college and I'm gonna be stuck here forever, taking care of people. Well, who's gonna take care of me?

Answer me soon,

Natasha

■

December 5, 1990
Natasha,

Snow's coming down outside the window, but it won't stick cause the sun too bright. New York ain't ready for old man winter I see, not ready to slow down for a change. Pretty soon the sun gonna fade and the snowflakes will stick and the snow will hide everything that's dirty about this place. I bet when it's covered with snow, this place look like a world of clouds—all peaceful and shit. Not at all hard and tough like we know it to be. I'm sorry to hear about your grandmother, I really am. I know you loved her a lot. I know you gonna miss her. I know Drew was real close to her since he lived with her and all for so many years. Tell youngun to keep his head up. I wish I could think of something more to say, something to make you feel better, but I can't. I hope you know that one person who do worry about you is me. I know that don't mean nothing cause it ain't shit I can do up here if something happen to you, but I think about you by yourself on the train at night coming home from work, think about you going to and from school all by yourself. I think about you not having the money to keep yourself looking good, like the Black Queen you are. I think about all that shit all the time, but it ain't nothing I can do about it and that really hurts me deep down inside. It hurts me deep to my core, to my manhood. It's hard to feel like a man when you can't take care of your woman.

That's why I'm going back to class, Natasha. That's why I'm not feeling sorry for myself no more. That's why I'm about to change and be brand-new. I gotta keep it together and keep my perspective straight. If it'll make you feel better, I'm going to get my job back. I'm saving my money so I can send you something real nice. You deserve the best and I'm gonna give it to you any way I can.

Love, your man,

Antonio

December 6, 1990

Antonio, well I took the test today. The SAT test I told you about I need to get into college. I went down there with Tamika and Valencia from the program. Valencia real religious, even though she act like a dyke sometimes, and she wear that Hail Mary statue around her neck all the time, so we said a prayer right before we all went in there to take the test. I really don't think I did too good. The math part was a little easier cause I had studied all that real hard, plus I guess Mr. Lombard

wasn't that bad of a teacher after all. There was so many
questions on the test I never finished every one in the
section. All them long hard words just started running
together and I didn't know what they meant, words like
titular, colloquialism, egregious, gregarious, litigious. I'm
thinking to myself I never seen these words in my life
and they were NOT on them vocabulary lists that I got
to study. The whole time I was taking the test, Tamika
wasn't paying attention and tapping her pencil and looking around the room and stuff. Me and Valencia kept
trying to keep her focused, but she ended up grabbing
her coat and walking out. The man who was giving us
the test had stopped her and said, "Ma'am, the test is not
over and if you leave now you won't be able to return to
the testing room," and she shouted, "I don't care. I'm
through with this. I'm up." So that was the end of that
for her. She gave up on herself and didn't even try to finish. I pushed on though, tried to make the best of it.

Monday Mr. Lombard come grabbing me in the hallway trying to talk to me about being in the program.
Dawg, I don't know why that man always trying to be
my friend. He was like, "Natasha, you're a feisty girl and
I sense you're a real go-getter. I think you should apply
to school out of New York State. I'll write you a recommendation." And I'm thinking, Yeah you gonna write
me a recommendation, but is you gonna pay for tuition?
I'm going right up there to City College like everybody
else cause a sister is ba-ROKE, okay? He gave me all
these pamphlets for all these schools I ain't never even

heard of. Brown and Stanford and Yale and Georgetown and University of Chicago. Georgetown was the only one I knew cause I watch their basketball team on TV sometimes. But it's way down there in D.C. I'm not leaving New York. I can't leave my mother, even though Mr. Lombard told me I should expand my horizons. Here's some of what he wrote about me in his recommendation: "Initially, Natasha's intelligence and maturity went unnoticed by me because she seemed to be trying to hide it behind a tough exterior and somewhat comic demeanor. Such a tendency is common in a school system such as ours, where academic excellence is not rewarded or acknowledged nearly as much as it should be. However, as the school year has progressed, Natasha's true personality and potential have emerged to reveal a very motivated and dedicated student. She has expressed a desire to learn above and beyond what she is being taught, and this initiating spirit is what has set Natasha apart from other students I teach." That's just a little of what he said. Nice, huh? I actually been helping him out in his classroom after school, and we don't even fight that much anymore.

Things is going well though at the house. Drew moved back with us so I ain't got my own room no more. Space is kinda tight, but he been real cool though, not bothering none of my posters or other shit I got on the wall. We gonna start moving Grandma and Granddaddy stuff out real soon. Mommy said she gonna sell the house. It'll be too much money to fix up—the sewage be backing up all the time, the roof leaks, the cabinets all old and rusted. She said she gonna sell it and keep the money for me, to buy me a car when I graduate high school or pay my tuition for college. I told her she needed to keep that money cause she was gonna need it to buy her big pretty house one day. Mommy said she was just fine where she was and right now her only concern is us, her kids. She finally decided to go back to work, and Roy actually been nice for a change. He been cooking and cleaning up and renting movies at Blockbuster. Maybe he really do love her, but just got a funny way of showing it.

Love,

Natasha

■

December 8, 1990

I'm back in class AND I got my J-O-B back! Ms. Harris convinced them to let me work again, so I got some income coming in. Video Soul on the TV. Sun shining outside. I benched 180 today. We had tacos for lunch. Shit is all good. Pretty soon, it's gonna be Christmas and almost one year I been in here. That's how I gotta live now—I don't count days, I count years. I know you did good on your test. You the smartest girl in the world. Shit, I don't know what I would have done all them times without you helping me with my homework. Hearing your voice the other night gave me a hard-on that wouldn't go away for hours. I had to count sheep so I could stop thinking about you.

Baby, we really ought to think about getting married right now and shit. I mean, why wait? You do love me, don't you? That way, we could see each other at least with them conjugal visits. I mean, it ain't much and it wouldn't be like living together, but we could go ahead and at least spend some time together. Matter of fact, we could even go ahead and get that family started. I mean, why wait? We can go ahead and have our shorties now so we can still be young when they growin up. Why don't we think about doing it this summer? It could be nice. I know what you thinking—that a wedding in jail is ghetto but really it's not. I asked Ms. Harris about this and she say you get a preacher, and you can wear a dress and I can take off my jumpsuit and put on a real suit so we can take a nice picture on our wedding day. I think we can even invite some people for witness, and I believe you get a cake. I mean, it's not the big old wedding on Long Island that we had talked about, but we could do that later. Think about it, baby. I need you and I don't want to wait anymore.

Love,
Antonio

December 16, 1990

Baby look, I ain't trying to bust your bubble or crumble your cookies, but you must be buggin if you think I'm

about to get married in a jail. Antonio baby, I'm sorry
and you know I love you and everything and I'm sticking
by you til the end, but that's just plain crazy. What we
gonna tell our kids? What I'm gonna tell my family? Oh
yeah, I'm getting married upstate but not how you
think? C'mon now. And you think I'm about to let you
knock me up while you still locked up? Who gonna get
up with them kids at night? While you all laid out and
slobbin and snorin like you do, it ain't gonna be nobody
but me and my mother and you know that shit is real.
Who gonna put clothes on the baby back and buy dia-
pers and milk? You? Antonio, you ain't even making
minimum wage at your job, so once again it's all gonna
be on me. Being a single mother ain't no joke. Believe
me, Laneice about to learn cause she done already called
me crying talking about Black fucked Sherry Thompson
last week. I'm not going through that. I see now it's a
whole big world out there just a plane ride away and I'm
gonna see it. I don't even know if I want to have kids in
New York. I want them to see something different,
something better than what I've seen. Like my kids ain't
getting on no subway, Michael Antonio Lawrence II. You
can forget it. You better have a good job so we can have
us a car. I see all these girls, walking around Harlem
without a man, waiting for somebody to stop and help
them get they baby stroller up and down the train steps.
That shit ain't cute. All them germs and homeless people
shitting on themselves and people coughing and shit
down there. Fuck that—my baby'll be dead in a few

months going down there. And I ain't taking NONE of my kids to no jail to see they daddy. That gotta be the worst thing in the world, to get to know your daddy behind bars, and I got too much love for any black baby in this world to see them go through that shit. Antonio, I got goals and dreams. I'm going to college and I ain't having no babies before I finish! That's it, end of story. You can forget it. You thinking with your dick and not your head. So you better just exercise your hands or hope for early release cause I'm not walking down the aisle in no jail. That's not how it's gonna be.

■

December 24, 1990

Natasha yo, why you gotta go and ruin a brother's Christmas and shit cause he trying to make plans with you, cause he trying to tell you how he feels and what's been on his mind? Why you gotta go and insult my manhood like that? You taking things way too serious kid, and that's on the real. You think I was being for real and that I don't know I can't provide for you or no shorties right now? You think I ain't aware of that? Damn Natasha, sometimes a brother wanna have some dreams, something to think about that I can share with you and shit, but you gotta be all smart and trifling. You done made me so mad I don't even wanna tell you I passed my GED. Yeah, that's right, I got an 85. But I guess that's not good enough in your book. It should have been 100. Merry Christmas with your trifling ass,

Antonio

■

December 26, 1990

Well Merry Christmas and Happy New Year and FUCK YOU TOO! Damn, I was just playing, you need to learn how to take a joke. God, it ain't that serious. Anyway, thank you for my card although you could have wrote something nasty or nice in it, but I guess you still mad so whatever. Did you get my Christmas card and the Adidas windpants I sent you? I hope the pigs let you have it, but I don't know how strict they are about the uniform. I mean, ain't no pockets or nuthin, so I don't see why they wouldn't let you wear em (at least to bed so you can get a woody in them when you smell the raspberry mist perfume I sprayed on em!). I thought the card I gave you was cute, with the little monkeys on the front dressed up like Santa Claus. I thought it might make you laugh. This Christmas was actually better than a lot of Christmases we had, even though Grandma was missing. I got a lot of stuff—clothes mostly. My biggest presents was some Guess jeans and a Starter coat. It's the L.A. Lakers even though I'm a New York girl, but Mommy know I like to wear bright colors—purple and yellow, my favorites. Drew got one too. I guess Mommy think that shit is cute for her kids to match, but she keep forgetting Drew is just a pitiful little seventh-grader and I on the other hand am a grand senior.

I used my discount to buy Mommy a lot of stuff we needed for the house—a knife set, a blender so we could make some Slim-Fast shakes cause we getting big, and a wok. I don't know what we gonna cook in the wok cause the only Chinese food I eat is shrimp fried rice, but it just seem fancy to say you got one. Roy bought her a gold necklace that had Grandma's initials on it: *E.P.* Earline Preston. It wasn't no herringbone but I guess it was cute. I took your mother present over last night. Remember I asked you if she would like some vanilla candles? Well, she loved em. She acted like they was some diamond earrings or something. That's cause I don't think nobody else got her nothing. Tyler gave her some Christmas ornaments he made in school, Styrofoam snowmen with pipe cleaners. They was hanging on the tree that was sitting on the television. She said her and her sisters don't never exchange gifts cause they too old for all that. She said she ain't seen Trevon in days. He probably got him a girlfriend or something somewhere. I mean he do got a little hair on his chest now and you know how y'all start acting with that hair on your chest. I think this year gonna be good, Antonio. For both of us, I hope.

Merry Christmas,

Natasha

PS. Congratulations boy on your GED. I KNEW YOU COULD!!!!!!

January 4, 1991

Okay Antonio, I don't know what's up with you, but you ain't wrote me back yet. Maybe you busy. Demands of the job? Got you working late, honey? Ha ha ha, I'm just joking trying to make you laugh. Anyway, when you get a minute hit me back. You can call me too cause for the next two weeks I'm bout to be at home all night working on all my applications. I got a one thousand on the SAT, that's a good enough job considering where I started. I'm gonna apply to ten schools cause I don't got to pay because of our income, which basically we ain't got. I'm even gonna apply to Columbia, although I know I ain't got a chance in hell of getting in that bitch. I don't know nobody from our school ever went there and it's damn near up the Hill. Well, gotta wrap this up cause I gotta make pork chops for dinner and I wanna do one application a night cause they all due this month. I might ask you to look over my essay—they call it a Personal Statement. Oh, and I think I'm gonna have to start talking proper and shit. Me and Tamika and Valencia been practicing cause if we go to college we gotta get that educated dialect together.

    Love,

    Natasha

PS. Your mother told me that Trevon been smoking up on the regular now, so you might wanna rap to him about his behavior. Oh, I mean Trevon has been smoking marijuana on a regular basis as of late, so you might want to confer with him about his mannerisms. That sounded good baby, didn't it?!?! Peace out!

■

January 11, 1991
Dear Antonio,

I'm having a really hard time writing my Personal Statement for college. Mr. Lombard said he would proofread it for me, but I don't know if I want him to see it. I mean, it is really, really personal. I really don't know what to say about what I want to do with my life. I feel like these people expect me to have all these great plans like wanting to be a doctor or a lawyer or something else, but all I'm really trying to do right now is survive. You get what I'm saying? I know you feel me. If anybody knows a thing or two about surviving, it's you. But here is what I think I'm gonna say. Lemme know what you think, if you like it or not.

Personal Statement
Natasha Riley

I don't know anybody who has ever been to college, so I haven't had anybody to tell me to go or talk to me about what it's like. My mother has always called me independent, headstrong, and even stubborn. So I believe my decision to want to go to college is an example of that in my personality. I realize that I might not have had the best education in the world. My school is very crowded, we don't even have books for half our classes, and most of the time the teacher doesn't even finish (or start) a lesson because the class is so rowdy. I used to be one of those rowdy kids who didn't care about school. When I lost my father about six years ago, I didn't think anything mattered anymore. But something came over me in the last few years that made me want to get serious about my future. I lost my grandmother who I had always been able to depend on, and my best friend in the whole world also went away. A light clicked in my head and I realized that in the end, I had to take care of myself. I decided that going to college is the first step for me to take in order to make sure I will be able to do that. To make up for not going to the best school, I read a lot on my own and I started studying every chance I got. I was also accepted into a special program that allowed me to visit France and leave America for the first time in my life. This program has been really demanding, with meetings on the weekend and after school, plus extra homework and studying. But I have done it and I feel very proud of that. I feel like my participation in this program and surviving some of the things I've had to go through means I can accomplish anything I set my mind to—including college. I know it won't be easy, but I believe in the end I have the potential to be one of the best students in your university.

■

January 15, 1991

Okay Antonio, I don't know what the hell is going on, what's wrong with you or what your problem is, but it's been three weeks since you wrote me back. What's wrong? Baby, talk to me. I hope you not still mad about what I said about us getting married in jail. Okay baby, fine if it's that serious and if it'll make you happy then we can go on ahead and get married in jail. I was just playing really I was. I would do anything for you. Anything.

Write back soon,
N

■

January 15, 1991

You would do anything for me, huh? Anything, you lying bitch? Anything like ride another man behind my back? Anything like lose my damn ring even though you probably threw it in the river cause you ain't wanna be bothered with me no more and didn't know how to say it? I know what you been doing. I know you been giving pussy to a nigga at your job. I know all about it. I know what kinda whip he pushin, where he live at, I even know he Jamaican. I know he be taking you out to eat after work and taking you to the movies and shit. I know you been staying out late with that nigga. Don't ask me how I know, I just know.

Why you had to lie to me? Why you had to make promises you know you wasn't gonna keep? Why you wrote me all these letters and shit telling me how much you love me and wanna be with me, but as soon as some faggot come along and hold a few dollars under your nose you forget all about that, huh? Typical female, that's all you are. You forget about me, about what we got, what we worked hard to build up. Benito say I should kill your ass, hold you down and look in your eyes and watch you bleed to death when I slit your throat. He said that's what he would do, and I believe he would. But I'm a better man than that. You ain't shit Natasha. You ain't shit. I wish I would have never met your ass.

January 18, 1991

So you found out about Roland, but baby I can explain. You ain't gotta tell me who told you cause I already know. Laneice told Black and Black told you, you ain't even gotta say it. And I can't even be mad at neither one of them cause she my friend, but that's her man, her baby's father, so she gonna tell him everything regardless. And you his boy, his best friend since third grade, so he gonna tell you everything regardless. But baby, Lane-ice got a tendency to exaggerate. I ain't been letting Roland take me out all the time. I swear I haven't. We only went to the movies one time and Apollo once to see TLC and he bring me stuff to eat at work all the time cause he get a longer break than I do cause he ain't part of sales floor, he part of security and it's a totally different company. And he really don't have to work there, he just banging and Macy's is a cover-up and I told him I didn't want no part of that. But anyway that's beside the point. I know you ain't gonna believe me, but I didn't fuck him. I swear that on my grandmother's grave. He wanted to and been asking me, but I won't let him cause I told him I'm in love with you. I told him me and you had something real, something special, and I didn't want to fuck it up.

Everybody been telling me to break up with you, but I can't. I can't leave you. I can't even think about it because all I see is you alone in that terrible place and I don't know, it just does something to my heart. I swear I didn't let him do me and if that's what you heard then that's a bald-faced lie. We kissed a little bit, that's all. I don't know what to say for myself except I was lonely and I was tired of being by myself all the time, hearing my girlz talk about niggas and I wasn't talking about nobody. I got tired of that. I know it was wrong and I know I shouldn't have even started kicking it with him and I promise I'm gonna stop. He bought me some new sneaks for Christmas and I wouldn't even accept them. I won't ever talk to him again. I'll even quit my job and get another one if you want me to. I'll do that for you. I promise I will. I don't even see him no more. He been on probation anyway at the job for his attendance. I can't tell you the last time I even saw him. Please don't be mad at me. You the only one ever been up in this I swear, and you the only one ever will. I promise that too. Baby, please don't ignore my letters. Write me back soon. You're the only one I love.

Love,
Natasha

■

February 1, 1991
Baby Girl,

Well Natasha, I been thinking a lot about the shit that went down, about you cheating on me and shit. About some other man on top of you with his stuff all inside of you, making you come. I been thinking about it real hard, so hard it make my head hurt and spots come in front of my eyes and I ain't been talking much.

I had to meet with Ms. Harris to talk about what I was gonna try to do as far as my education while I was in here, and I guess I wasn't doing nothing but hunching my shoulders and nodding cause she told me, Something's bothering you and you're obviously not in a position to think clearly because of it. I told her, Ain't nothing wrong with me that ain't been wrong. And she said, I've gotten to know you very well over the last few months, and you definitely seem different. So I told her about you and what you did. I told her about you creeping behind my back, with somebody who probably look better than me and can put it down better than me. I told her about him having a real job and being able to buy you real shit, not just cards and whatever. I started crying and shit, something I ain't done in a minute, and I was embarrassed to do it in front of her. But she helped me get myself together, put my head on straight. She basically spit the truth at me, the truth I hadn't been wanting to face. She was like, Antonio it seems that you and your fiancée are both still very young and have a lot of living to do. Antonio, be honest with yourself. Do you really see this relationship surviving nine more years? I tuned her out, shut my ears and eyes just by thinking the same way I used to when Daddy hit my moms cause I was feeling all hot and red the way I did that day when I threw my files on the floor, and I didn't want to get in trouble again. But she couldn't let the issue die. She just kept on going and going . . . Antonio, your fiancée sounds like a very smart, beautiful girl and I'm pretty sure it's hard for her to live out her young adulthood without dating or any male interaction. A woman has many needs, Antonio . . . I just had to cut her off at that point cause she was making it seem like I did something wrong. So I just snapped back, Let's just get off me and get back to college cause I shouldn't be discussing my personal bizness with you anyway and I don't know why I expected you to listen. I should have known you would have taken her side cause you a woman and you all gonna stick together so let me let you get back to what you do best. Then she started that brother shit again. Hold on now brother don't get mad at me because I'm trying to give you a woman's perspective, this isn't my fault and I'm only trying to help you. I told her I didn't need no help I needed my life back, I needed my woman back, I needed high school back, I needed my boyz back, I needed hugs from my mother back, and if she couldn't give me that she couldn't help me. She changed the subject then, and told me, Well, I'm gonna leave your personal "biz" alone and let you deal with that on your own. I'm only going to ask that you think about at least some of what I said. But by then, my time was up so we couldn't talk about shit anyway.

Well, she did put something on my head. She was right, Natasha. She was right. We ain't gonna make it. I mean, we don't see each other. We can't share a slice of pizza or get a cherry bomb from Mister Softee together no more. We can't go to the movies or chill in front of the TV or watch Nick at Nite on the phone together all night. We can't hold each other and talk about all the things we want to do in life. We can't make each other feel good the way a man and woman supposed to make each other feel good. We can't do none of that and without that we ain't got shit. I'm nothing but a bunch of letters in a box and a few pictures on the wall to you. I'm nothing but a bunch of memories and pictures floating around your head, weighing you down.

That's all I am. Well, you way more than that to me. I forgive you for cheating. I guess. I still want to try to work on the relationship, I still want to get married and stuff when I get out of here. But I understand how you feel and what you going through because I'm going through it too, maybe more than you. The shit ain't easy. So check this out. If you feel like you need to hook up with other brothers from time to time in order to satisfy your needs then go ahead and do that. I'll give you permission. I just don't want to know about it. Keep that shit to yourself so I won't have to think about it or imagine it in my head. I know you might think I'm crazy by letting you get away with all that, but I just don't know what else to do. I need somebody to love me, I need to feel like it's a reason for me to get up and go through the motions every day. You my reason and I'll do anything to keep you. I need you. You keep me sane. I can't live without you. So do what you got to do. Just remember who really loves you.

    Antonio

February 25, 1991
Antonio,

I know it's been a while, baby, since we spoke. We both forgot about Valentine's Day. I didn't know what to say to you about my actions. I talked to my mother about you—about us. She told me that if we really love each other, we can get through anything. Even distance and time. I want to believe that what we have is that strong. Did you get my birthday card? Sorry it was late. I just been real busy. A lot of stuff happened since you found out about me and Roland. Me and Ms. Clark been shopping a lot for Laneice. We giving her a baby shower at her aunt's house out on Long Island and so we been getting decorations and stuff. Plus, me and Mommy gonna be looking for houses pretty soon. She got into that program I was telling you about, the one where we can get a real house to call our own. Well, not a house, but you know what I mean. An apartment, somewhere real nice. So she been telling everybody in our family and we been going out to Jersey to the outlets to get pretty stuff, real nice stuff that deserve to be in a nice house. Pretty bright pillows and soft rugs and curtains with flowers on them.

Well, I guess the real reason I haven't answered your letters is I just figured you was real mad at me and I didn't really want to aggravate it. I DID NOT DID NOT DID NOT let Roland hit it. I promise I didn't give it up to him, even though you right, maybe I wanted to. But I ain't interested in seeing other guys or sleeping with nobody else. That's not the main thing I think about. I guess the truth is, Antonio, that I want to go somewhere in my life. I really want to bounce out of New York, go somewhere different for a change, see something else. Mommy say I can do anything I want to do if I try hard enough and really put my mind to things. I been thinking lately about how much I liked to read books and write and stuff. I mean, I would rather write letters to you all day than do any real work. So I been looking into some schools where I can do that, maybe be a journalist or something like that. And some of these schools ain't in New York, so I won't be able to come see you and feel like I got a real man when I'm gonna be so far away. And I'm not gonna have the time and stuff either. I mean, we did this time management workshop in one of the seminars we gotta go to for my college prep program. They gave us this calendar with all these time slots for every hour on them, and they gave us a fake class schedule. It was like this: I had French class three times a week, English 101 three times a week, College Algebra twice a week and I had to pick a elective for three times a week. I was thinking about taking up something fun like dance since that's what I like to do in my free time and you know I'm good at that. Member the last home-coming dance we went to, before all this shit broke us up, and how everybody was around me and Laneice in a circle and we was punking everybody who stepped to us and you and Black was the only ones who could handle it? So I was thinking maybe I could be a writer and a choreographer too. But back to the exercise, I had to have a work-study job for fifteen hours a week, house meetings in the dorm once a week, plus exercise at the gym cause I ain't trying to get fat in college, three hours of study time every day, and one activity which I think is gonna be either student government or the black students group. Definitely the black student organization cause you know I gotta be down for my people. Well, when I filled out the chart I didn't hardly have no time left for myself. I was bugging out cause I was thinking, when am I gonna get to sleep? I mean, I probably won't even have as much time as I want to come back to New York and see my mother in her new house. I'm not saying I wanna break up or nothing, I'm just saying maybe we should just take a break for a while. Lemme know what you think about that. I gotta go cause I hear Roy bitching cause I didn't wash the dishes and I ain't trying to have him tell Mommy that shit when she get home and ruin her day. I'll talk to you later, I guess.

Love,

Natasha

■

March 14, 1991

Natasha baby, I take back everything I ever said about us breaking up. I take back everything I ever said about not wanting us to be together. The truth is right now I feel like I'm going crazy. I feel like I'm losing my mind thinking about you all the time. I can't take it. I don't want to do nothing but walk around my room and hit the walls cause I get so mad I can't stop thinking about not being with you. I remember the first time I saw you. You was coming up from the 2 train on 135th, with your long braids in a big ponytail on top of your head coming down over your face.

You had on that pink baby doll top with your little white Pumas on to match, these tight yellow leggings on showing off them Coke-bottle hips. Your face was shining cause of sweat but to me your face looked liked the world's only black sun. I remember I had sucked in my breath and I think I stopped breathing for a minute cause I thought you was so cute. That was about five, six years ago, and I thought I wouldn't never see you again then we wind up at the same high school. That mean something. That must be fate and mean we need to be together.

Check this out. I will do anything I can to be with you, even break out of here if I have to. And I don't care who seeing this or reading this cause I just want to show you how much I love you and how much I need you and care about you. I'll do anything for you, Natasha. Anything. Just please don't leave me, don't break up with me now. I will kill myself. Believe me when I say I will do that shit and it'll be all your fault. Don't do this baby. Don't do this to me. I'll call you later. I love you baby.

Antonio

■

March 16, 1991

I don't know where you been, but I been calling your house and you ain't been answering so I don't know what's going on. I'll just wait on your letter. I know it's coming. I know you just handling your biz right now. Life goes on on the outside. I ain't stupid. I know me being in here don't stop the world. So you go ahead and do everything you gotta do. I'll just wait for you to be home when I call. Write me back as soon as you get this.

Antonio

■

March 21, 1991

Okay, so now I know something wrong. You ain't bothering to take none of my calls and I know what time you be at home. I know that somebody been picking up the phone and saying they don't want to accept the charges. You trying to avoid me now. Is that it? You don't love me no more? Don't know how to be a woman and tell me woman to man? What's next? You gonna put your moms or Roy on the phone to tell me the truth? Well I'm not having this shit, Natasha. I'm not gonna take this bullshit from you. I'm not gonna let you get away from me. You can forget about that. Don't you hear me at night in your dreams, calling out your name in the dark? I know you can hear me. I know you can feel what I feel. Don't leave me. Don't do this to me. Don't pretend like you don't hear me whispering your name.

Your man forever,
Antonio

March 26, 1991

I hope you hear the bang when I blow my brains out over you. Don't think I can't get a piece up in here cause I can. There are ways. Believe me, there are ways. So I hope you hear it while you all curled up, warm in your bed, without a care in the world, hugging one of your stuffed bears or maybe even another nigga for all I know cause obviously I don't know you like I think I did. I hope you happy and I hope you can taste my blood in your mouth and feel it splattered all over your face bitch.

March 28, 1991

Look Antonio, it's over. I thought I was strong enough to deal with this, but I'm not. I can't take it no more. You told me you didn't care if I saw other guys, but there is no way I can do that to you because I care about you too much. No matter what you say, I know that would hurt and the last thing I want to do is hurt you more than you've already been hurt. Baby, it's not you I promise it's not. It's just been almost a year and a half since you been locked up and I want a life. I want a real normal life like other girls my age. Stop calling here twenty times a day. Stop sending me so many letters cause I don't have time to write back. Stop lying to your mother and telling her all these lies about me. She hates me now.

Do you know she came over here? Do you know she barged up into our house demanding to know what I did to you? I told her, "I ain't do nothing to Antonio. I just told him I wanted to break up, that's all." Then she said, "You little heifer, it's cause of you that he lost his mind and started screaming and tearing up things and had to be put away all by hisself and alone. It's because of you." So luckily my mother was home cause it seemed like your moms wanted to hit me or kill me or something. My mother came out from the back, curlers all in her hair and everything, like "Hold on, what's going on out here?" When your moms tried to explain, Mommy didn't even let her finish. She just said, "Look, you don't got a right coming up in here blaming Natasha for Antonio's problems." Your mother said something like, "I'm not blaming Natasha for nothing. I just wish she would quit playing games with my son. This shit ain't a game and she needs to understand that if she don't want nothing to do with him then she needs to leave him the fuck alone." So my mother got all big and bad up in her face and said, "Now wait a minute, honey, you wait just a minute. You in my house and I will not allow you to come up in here disrespecting me or my daughter. If you wanna be out of line you better do it outside the door." I mean, I thought they was about to brawl. But it didn't happen like that. I don't know what happened, your mother just started crying. Right there in front of us, she just started screaming real loud and wouldn't stop and she said something like, "At least you got your baby right here with you. Don't nobody love me. Don't nobody think about what I been through." Then my mother hugged her, hugged her real tight like everybody did for her when Grandma died. She hugged her until I thought they both was gonna fall over. Then my mother sent me out of the room. She told me to go to the back or go outside so they could talk.

I went back to my room, but I still heard them a little bit. I heard my mother trying to tell her that this thing was hard on everybody, not just her, and that she heard me sometimes crying in the middle of the night over this whole thing. I didn't know she knew about that. I didn't think nobody knew how I felt about things, not even you. I probably should have told you how I felt sooner. I probably shouldn't have let things go on as long as they did. That's my bad and I'll go ahead and accept that responsibility. Maybe I did lead you on too far. And maybe that was wrong. But I did—no, I still do—love you. And it's hard to let go of somebody you love. Believe me, it ain't been as easy as you think. I promise that I still love you, and that we'll be friends forever and ever and ever. And who knows, maybe we will get married one day. I don't know, Antonio. I just don't know. But I can't keep on living a lie cause I'm scared you gonna try to kill yourself. I can't lie to you and tell you I want to be with you now, but I can't feel like I'm in a prison either.

And nobody, not you or your mother or my friends or no-body else, gonna make me feel guilty about my decision. You not being fair lying to your mother and telling her I'm the reason you snapped. Antonio, if you kill yourself, that's on you. That's gonna be your mistake. Don't try to make me feel like it's mine.

Natasha

■

April 11, 1991

Hi Antonio. I know I told you I didn't want to be hooked up no more, but I just want to make sure we're still friends, still cool. Antonio, I do care about you. Well anyway, Laneice had her baby as I'm sure you heard. A little girl she named Sharon Angelique Clark. I think that's a real pretty name. Sharon. You don't hear names like that no more. Well, here's a picture of her if you care. She's pretty, ain't she, even though her eyes is shut? She a redbone just like Black. How did he ever get the name Black anyway, with his high yellow ass? He didn't come to the hospital when the baby was born. He was some-where drunk and high with his boys. When he did fi-nally show up at the hospital, Mr. and Mrs. Clark didn't even speak to him. But back to Laneice. She seem like she gonna be a real good mom. I mean, she keep herself busy with that baby, don't put it off on her mother or nothing, not that Mr. Clark would be having that anyway. She seem happy about it, I guess. I even asked her one day if she was happy. We was sitting in her room. I was helping her put baby lotion and powder all over Sharon, then we wrapped her up in this real cute pink and white striped onesy from the Gap. It was really sunny outside and the Softee truck was out and the bikers was out and you could hear all the music from the cars going by. I felt like I could taste summer and I couldn't wait to get out. But Laneice ain't gonna be able to get out too much with that baby. She was like, "Yeah girl, I love Sharon. Now that she here, I wouldn't give her back for the world. I don't care what happen between me and Black. I'm never gonna wish her back." I think she kind of know that Black might not stick around. I mean, he only about seventeen or eighteen. Look at us. We thought we was gonna be together and look what happened. So she don't have her head in the clouds about that. It's good she know she might have to do it with or without him. I just said, "Wow, that's sweet to give up so much for somebody else." Then she told me, "No, it ain't sweet. It just is what it is. I don't even think about it like I'm giving up nothing. Things just gotta change a little bit, that's all." She said that she still gonna try to finish high school. I told her she might as well since this our last year and all. That girl always hated school, so she probably just gonna get her GED.

But Black seem like he gonna try to stick around. He over there so much Mr. Clark had to tell him to go home one day. Mr. Clark said he might be able to get Black a job with his car service, or in Madison Square Garden cause he got a brother who a supervisor over there. I might as well tell you my plans. I'm gonna go away to college. I got into some really good schools, Antonio. I got into Rutgers and City College and this school in Boston and one way out in Chicago, Illinois. All the schools gave me financial aid and everything. I mean, I'm gonna have to have some loans, but they gave me a lot of scholarship too. I told Mr. Cook and I swear I ain't never seen that man smile the way he did when I told him my good news. He asked about you. I told him you was doing alright. I didn't tell him we broke up though.

Tamika want me to go to this junior college in Jersey so I can be her roommate cause that's where she going, and Valencia pulling my arm to go to Stony Brook out on Long Island so I can be her roommate there. She got into this fancy school, Brown, but she don't want to go too far from her family and her man Pito, which I can understand. One school called the University of Chicago is kinda related to the program I been doing, so I think that's how I was able to get in there. They got this summer program for kids like me, I guess kids who didn't come from great schools and who gonna need a little help before college. But if I went there and did this program, I would have to leave in June and be there for the whole summer. I never been to Chicago or anywhere that far so I decided that I think I want to go there. I think I'm ready for an adventure. I need a change. Maybe it'll help me clear my mind. Mommy been crying and making me feel all guilty. She been talking about, "I don't want you going all the way to no Chicago leaving me all by myself." I told her, "Mommy, this is my decision and I'm gonna do it. We'll just have to talk on the phone a lot, and if I don't like it I'll come home." But I told her I wanted to go and at least try. She don't say nothing, just keep on crying saying, "I don't care. I don't like it, I don't like it." Well, I like the idea of me doing something I want to do. Something on my own. Something . . . something for Natasha.

Love always,

Natasha

PS. I will try to come up and see you before I leave. I don't know when cause I'm going to be working a lot to save up money. But I promise, I'll try.

■

May 16, 1991
Natasha,

So you really going, huh? I guess I didn't really believe you at first, but when I saw you last weekend you looked so different I knew it had to be something to make that big of a change in you. I mean, you just looked more mature, I guess, with your new Halle Berry haircut and your nice sweater. You looked good in that corny schoolteacher gear, so I guess you gonna fit right in in college. Guess you just get-

ting better with time, which is the way it's supposed to be. Benito and Mohammed been calling me old man lately, say I done changed and got all quiet and they even showed me some lines around my eyes that wasn't there before. I guess that's the way it is when you see everything slipping away. I still been going to my job. It's cool. Me and Ms. Harris been looking into some correspondence courses that I might be eligible for. She told me that it was certain things I probably wouldn't do cause of my background she call it. Like anything in education or working with animals or whatever would be hard for me to do cause I been convicted of a violent crime. I'm a felon for life, baby. I won't be able to shake that shit. When I get out of here, I'm gonna tell you the truth about what happened that night and why I'm really here. Everybody thinks they know the truth about me, but they really don't. Including you. I'll just ask you again what I asked you before: Do you really believe I killed my father? Do you really believe it went down the way it did?

I guess it doesn't matter at this point. But I'm just glad you feel good about yourself and things you got ahead of you. Natasha, you don't ever wanna feel like this. You wanna always keep them bright eyes and that bushy tail like MGD used to say about me. You don't ever wanna go through what I been through, feel like I feel every day when I wake up. You feel like faded graffiti on a building they bout to tear down—something a man worked hard on to try to make the world a more beautiful place, and nobody *appreciated it. Or cracked glass in the street that used to be something pretty, but the cars keep driving over it like it never really mattered or was never anything whole and real. But I guess you wouldn't know nothing about that. Or maybe I'm wrong. Maybe you would.*

Don't forget me,
Antonio

PART FOUR

November 26, 1991
Antonio,

I'm home on my Thanksgiving break and I come back to find out your moms and mine is like best friends and shit now. They be going shopping and to the beauty shop and to the movies together. I thought I would give this letter to your mother to send. I couldn't come to New York and not go by and say hi to your mother. She got your GED on the wall and in a real nice frame, right next to that picture we took the first time we came to visit you up- state. She's looking really good, Antonio. Lost a little bit of weight, had her hair fixed up real nice. She said she's been going to the Y to work out. She said she's about to start working at this day care center in the mornings. I can't believe somebody broke in your spot. Your mother told me all about it. They took Tyler's Nintendo, the TV, the VCR, some of the leather out the closet.

But I guess you know about all that. I mean she is your mother and this is still your house. I guess you wanna hear about me and mine. Drew is all right, getting ready to go to high school. Mommy's cool. She been spoiling me since I got home. I swear I never ate so much macaroni and cheese in my life, she keep stuffing it down my throat cause she know it's my favorite. I eat at the cafeteria at school, and I swear to God them people need to learn a thing or two about cooking. I lost so much weight cause I don't eat at that place, except for cereal and salad. I mean, one time, they had fried chicken covered in corn meal. C'mon now. Called it "Southern baked" or some shit. Them white and Chinese folks was tearing it up though.

So you wanna know about college? It's cool. I got four classes: French, this class called Humanities where basically you read a lot of old books, precalculus, and physical sciences. That's a lot of weird shit, huh? My roommate is this white chick from Oregon named Sarah. I didn't even know where Oregon was until I met her. She a real cool punk-rocker type, just kinda messy and hooked up with a scraggly-looking white boy who wanna rap. He got dreadlocks with yarn twisted in em. They look real nasty but I guess she likes it cause every night I come home she got a sock on the door—her way of telling me they doing it and I gotta go hang somewhere else for a minute. One night they gonna try to do it while I was in the room, cause I heard the bed squeaking a little bit and all their punk-rocker chains jingling and whatnot. I checked them on that shit real fast. I was like, "I don't get down like that, keep your business behind closed doors and we gonna get along real good." That's the only beef we ever had and now we kinda friends, if you can believe that. We stay up late at night talking, her telling me about the ocean and me telling her about New York. We stay up late studying a lot too.

It's a lot harder than I thought. We don't have semesters here like at regular colleges, we have quarters which make it a little bit harder because that means we have finals and midterms three times a year instead of twice. When I got here and saw all these people and all this grass and ivy climbing up the sides of the building, all I could think was, "What the hell am I doing here?" I felt dumb and poor, walking around with my raggedy book bag from high school when these people rocking leather briefcases. I spent a lot of time crying on the phone with Mommy and Laniece and Valencia and Tamika. They all said the same thing, basically, this is what I wanted so now I just gotta make the best of it. At first, it was weird cause the classes all small and the teachers don't just get up and talk to us like I thought. It's like fifteen people in the class. I'm the only black face and everybody talking all proper about philosophy and shit. So I had to step up my game a lot. Then I didn't want to talk cause I didn't want nobody figuring out my accent and asking me where I was from, and when I say Harlem they gotta ask me all these questions about crack and drive-bys and shit. I got so sick and tired of telling people it wasn't all like what you see on TV. We got doctors and lawyers and teachers and bus drivers and just hardworking people trying to make it in our neighborhood. It ain't all gutter. I had to remember what my mother told me when we got here and didn't see one black face the whole time: "You just as good as anybody here and don't you forget it." I never thought it was gonna be easy, but I don't think I ever did so much reading and writing in my life.

I like Chicago a lot. It's a little boring, not as much stuff going on. People talk real country out here—I thought I was in Alabama when I got off the plane. You can't get pizza on every corner, and when you do get pizza it's not sliced thin but it's real fat. They call it stuffed. It's real clean though, no dog shit and chicken bones all over the sidewalk like it is in Harlem. They got a train, most of them are els like in the Bronx and Brooklyn. I been to the downtown a few times. It looks like 5th Avenue a little bit with all the stores, and they got this place called Garrett's Popcorn that got the best cheese popcorn I ever tasted in my life.

But I'm glad about that cause then I can keep my mind on what's important. They gave me a little scholarship cause we really ain't got much family income, but I got loans and I'm not trying to waste all this money.

Laneice looking real good. She's trying to get an apartment in the Bronx across the 3rd Avenue Bridge, where it's a little cheaper. She said she can't afford Harlem no more, especially since her and Black ain't together. Did he tell you about that? He's going with some Mexican girl from Brooklyn. Laneice say he spending so much time deep in Sunset Park that he barely even make it up to Harlem to see her and the baby anymore. That's a damn shame. He really seemed like he was for real too. Glad it's not me. She said her parents wanted her to stay with them but she knew it was time for her to get out on her own. One of her cousins wanted her to come stay in Drew Ham with her, but Laneice said she would rather

have a tiny studio in the Bronx than live in the projects
in Harlem. I screamed, "Bitch what happened to us being Harlem Chicks 4 life?" and she said, "How you
gonna talk about me bitch when you moved 800 miles
away?" I told her I'm coming back, I can't leave for too
long. Just had to be up for a little while to better myself.
But I know where my home is and I'm coming back to it.
Well, this letter is getting a little long. My new address
is on the envelope. Hit me back when you get a chance.

Love,

Baby Girl

PS. Antonio I just want to make sure you know that
what happened between us was never about you. It was
always love. Life just got in the way.

■

December 12, 1991
Hey Baby Girl,

*Thought I'd wait about two weeks before I wrote back to
you, so then you would know I ain't no stalker and shit. I'm
shocked you gave me your address at college. I thought about
calling your moms and trying to get it, but then I thought
about it and I didn't want to cramp your style. I mean, you
probably got cats' tongues dropping to the floor out there in
Chicago, fresh new meat, Harlem girl with a body out of
this world. So I didn't want one of your boyfriends seeing a
letter from the pen sitting on your desk and shit. I know you*

ain't trying to broadcast the fact that your man in high school got locked up for doing some stupid shit that he can't even tell you how much he regret. It sound like you doing real good for yourself. Don't worry. This ain't the part where I'm gonna ask you back. I pretty much know that shit ain't gonna happen. I'm surprised we made it as long we did, and that's on the real. I was lucky to have you, and I fucked that shit up. I fucked a lot of shit up.

I didn't know about the break-in at my crib. My moms told me everything though after I got your letter and confronted her about it. She said she didn't want me in there worrying about nothing. I told her Ma, just cause I ain't there don't mean you ain't gotta tell me about what's going on. When Daddy died I officially took Daddy's place, so that meant I had to be the man of the house best way I could. She told me that her and Tyler was there by themselves when it went down and she was so scared she just couldn't get out the bed. When they come up here for that family Christmas shit they give us every year, I'm gonna make sure I set Trevon straight. I ain't gonna hit him, I can't hit him cause that'll be my ass and keep me further and further from getting out of here and back where I belong. But I'm gonna stare him down like he was my worst enemy and tell him he better clean up his act. That he better stop disrespecting Ma and living the life and stand tall and be a man until I can get back and look out for him. I swear to you, Natasha, I'm gonna put the fear of God in that little nigger if it's the last thing I do. Ma told me not to worry about it, but I can't not worry about it. She's right, it ain't shit I can do about nothing on the outside. Mo-

hammed said he got contacts on my block and could try to hook it up to find out who did it. I told him to do that shit. I might not be there to be the man of my house and protect my family the way I should, but I can damn sure make sure a nigga know not to fuck with me and mine.

But I know you don't want to hear all that. Here I go sounding like a gangsta, and you sounding all educated. Guess that just go to show that me and you is worlds apart right now. Most education I'm gonna get is some bullshit certificate in, I don't know, medical transcription or some other bullshit. It would have never lasted. Deep down inside I think I knew that, but I had to hold on to something. And I wanna thank you for sticking it out as long as you did. I wouldn't have survived a year in here without being able to think about you belonging to me. That's real. That's love. But I'm gonna let you go. I bet you got studying and shit to do. Study hard for me Natasha. I guess for all of us who didn't make it as far as you will. You gonna be somebody real important one day. I knew that the first time I laid eyes on you.

Love,
Antonio

December 22, 1991
Hey Antonio,

Just a little card to say Merry Christmas and let you know I was thinking about you. I'm home for about three weeks. I go back the first week in January. I finished up the semester with a B- average, which is fine in my book. I did the best I could and that's all you can ask for. Your mother asked me if I wanted to come up there for the party they give for the inmates and their families on Christmas, but I don't know, I just thought it wouldn't be appropriate, I guess. I mean, I don't know if you wanna see me like that. Sides, I gotta help Mommy move. She finally found a house that would accept her under this special Homeowner Program. She gonna get a renovated apartment in one of those buildings on 110th Street, brand-new and totally redone. Yep, 110th Street, right near Central Park. They got nice white walls, nice wood floors, a terrace and everything. She was already pretty much packed when I got here cause she so ready to get out of this building. I was there when the old white lady from the bank came over so she could sign all the papers to say the apartment was really hers. The lady called it closing on the house. Mommy was so excited that she could barely hold the pen to sign her name. It took her five minutes just to write her signature cause she said she couldn't believe it. "Less than ten years ago I was homeless, now I'm about to be a homeowner," she kept saying over and over. Her and Roy gonna get married, she told me. I wish she wouldn't cause I don't like him too much and Drew hate him, but she told me we just gonna have to live with it. She said he trying, and I guess he is. He stopped smoking and this guy he knows got him into the metal union, so he could be making like forty thousand dollars a year. Mommy always said to get a man with money, so I guess now that Roy gonna get some she better able to put up with his bullshit. But I'm running out of space and all I wanted to say was Merry Christmas. Have fun with your family.

Happy Holidays,
Natasha

■

December 22, 1991
Hey Natasha,

I know you probably at home on your winter break so I thought I would just send you a Christmas card to your mom's place, let you know I was thinking about you and you'll always be in my heart. No matter what happens. I don't know if you remember, but every year they have a Christmas party for us on Christmas Eve. You know, the ones of us that's had good behavior, which would definitely be me. I mean, it's actually kinda whack. They just have a little bit of food and some cake and punch and this Santa Claus and people donate toys for the little kids that come. But it's kind of fun cause people just chill and relax. So I don't know what you doing. I mean, you probably gonna be with your family and everything on that day so you can't come. But if you don't have anything to do and you don't mind the bus ride, you can come on up if you want. I mean, just let my mother know so I can put you on the list, and we can lie and say you my sister or some shit. But you might not get this in time anyway to know about it. If I don't see you, have a really nice Christmas. I hope you get everything you want.

Love,
Antonio

■

March 14, 1992
Hey Antonio,

Right now, I'm in this place called L'Hôtel Coulincourt in Montmarte in Paris. Yeah, I came back. I got accepted for the Université de Paris. I wanted to stay the whole year, but you KNOW my moms wasn't going for that. Plus, it costs a lot of money and I couldn't afford it. I still *parle français*. I'm getting much better and I even can write a whole paper in French. Never thought I'd be able to do that. I have two other people in my room, so I don't have a lot of privacy. I made friends with this one chick named Audrey. She's from this country in Africa called Liberia, but her father is this rich businessman. She showed me pictures of their house and I was like what? Africa got it like that? I wish I would have known that when I was in school and used to make fun of the African kids for the way they dressed and the way they talked. But this is the type of stuff you learn when you get out and see the world. And guess what? It's only one bathroom with a toilet and this little shower hose with a small curtain, and that's way in the hallway. Every room on the floor use that one bathroom. I guess they get down nasty like that in France. But besides that, I'm having fun. I'm getting to see a lot more than I got to see before. It's so many Africans here. If you thought the Africans has 116th down on lock in Harlem, you ain't seen nothing til you been out here. I mean, it's like everywhere you look you see coal-black people wearing the brightest colors you ever wanna see in your life. Me and Audrey be walking around, [skipping class quiet as it's kept,] looking at all the cute guys and she be like, "Oh yeah, he's Ethiopian" or "That can only be an Algerian nose," or "Girl, you can tell by the way he walks that he's Senegalese." I guess being out here and hanging out with people like Audrey, I really realize that I don't know much about the world. But I'm glad I'm finally learning.

Peace out,

Natasha

■

March 21, 1992

Hey Harlem Globetrotter,

I'm glad that some of us is seeing a little bit of the world. One thing I know about my world is that it never seems to change. Ma let one of her brothers stay with them cause he was down on his luck. Well, he had the balls to be slanging rock out of the crib. Somebody snitched, so NYPD's finest came in with a

search warrant. The best part is the motherfucker wasn't even
there. Popos tossed grenades and threw my mother down on the
living room floor, she told me. Thing is, Trevon knew all
about the dealing and let the shit go on in Ma's house anyway
cause he was getting a cut. Now, my uncle is hiding out somewhere. Where I can't say for obvious reasons, but he ain't coming back to Harlem no time soon. I been passing time, reading.
Black got him a job with the MTA. He said he through
playing games, dogging Laneice, dodging his responsibilities.
She don't want shit else to do with him. I can't blame her, and
I told Black that. We been friends long enough so that I ain't
gotta mince words with him. She handling business on her
own while he living the good life. Something ain't right about
that, even I know that from the fucked-up place where I sit.
But like all of us, he had to live and learn. He said he gonna
help me out with these correspondence courses I want to take.
He had to pay $400 upfront and then it's like twenty dollars
a month. I had told him I was interested in doing it, getting
at least a associate's degree and changing my life and coming
out here with at least something to show. He was sitting across
from me, holding up pictures of Sharon to the glass and shit.
When he told me he would do that for me, I couldn't believe it.
I was like, Yeah I can come out with a college degree, but I
won't be able to vote. He laughed and said, Motherfucker
your ass wasn't gonna vote no damn way. I was like True
that. And I started crying—not a lot, just a little—cause I
was thinking this is a true brother, this is a road dawg till
the end. He's quality. He about to take food out his baby's
mouth so I can get my shit proper, and I just broke down right

in front of him. I didn't care though. I ain't ashamed of showing my feelings anymore cause maybe if I would have before I wouldn't got in this mess. So I'm in college too. Wish I could be doing some of the things you're doing, but something better than nothing, right?

Love,

A

■

April 29, 1992

Yo Natasha,

Just writing to you to see what your world look like right about now. Shit is crazy out in L.A. Yo, you see that shit on the news? over there White cops beat Rodney King ass and they get off for that shit?!?! Every nigga up in here bout to explode. We on lock. Can't nobody leave the cell. Food brought to us. They locked us up over that shit, turned off the TVs, took the newspapers. You know Mohammed can't live without his newspaper or his news so he started screaming, Pigs keep the black man illiterate! Pigs keep the black man illiterate! Over and over and over again. I told him, Mohammed man, shut the fuck up—you don't want to get it. He just hunched his shoulders and told me, Tony my brother, they can't take our information, they can't take our information. But you know who got the upper hand in here, you know who gonna win. They came and took him away and I haven't seen him since.

Antonio

May 16, 1992
Dear Natasha,

*Well baby I'm gonna be a movie star. It's kinda wild I had
to get sent up for somebody to want me in a movie. This
white guy is making a documentary about life behind bars
or some shit like that. He came through the prison with the
warden and a video crew, looking for people to interview.
Most cats suspicious of that shit so they avoided him. Mohammed pulled me away and said be skeptical about white
people who always want to tell our stories so they can make
a profit, but they never want to live our lives. He called it
"exploitation" and spit at the cameraman when he came by
us in the yard. The guards ambushed him and took him
away, and Mohammed was just laughing the whole time.
This is his third violation in less than a month. He got
thirty days in solitary. Mohammed puts on this act like he
know it all, like nothing can break him. But I think he's finally cracked, finally let the power of the "man" crush him
like footsteps destroy a blade of grass struggling through a
crack in the sidewalk. One of his partners from his brother-
hood been quietly slipping me notes in the yard, crazy shit
Mohammed been writing on toilet paper and in blood cause
you can't have no privileges where he at. This time, they
threw him down in "The Farm"—not that regular hole
shit. The Farm makes the hole look like pre-school. One
shower A WEEK, one meal a day, no yard, no phone, no
books, no letters, no windows, no words with anybody but*

the devils playing around in your head. Cats do pushups and situps to pass the time, then it hits them like a ton of bricks that there are only so many of those you can do before you kill yourself. And then they start thinking about doing that, I've heard. That was my first detail on my first job, cause only prisoners with rank can escape that shit. I had to wear a mask, it stank so bad down there. They keep all the crazies down there, the mentals, the motherfuckers who've crossed the point of no return and just don't give no fuck anymore. The c.o. on duty got to be ready to face any-thing—darts they make out of material they find in the walls or on the floors, shit, piss, spit, throw-up. The last note Mohammed wrote said: I'm dying young blood. Nothing to look at but four walls and a small square of light. My ears have become my eyes. Grown men crying cursing, doors opening, chains rattling, foot-steps walking. That's all I have to let me know I'm not alone on this planet. That and the whisper of my own regrets. *I stayed up all night thinking about him, Natasha. Mohammed's been my ally since day one, and there ain't shit I can do for him now. I wrote him back on toilet paper and gave up 20 bucks of commissary for a c.o. to get it to him. I just reminded him of the time when he was grilling me about a higher power and I told him I didn't know if I believed in God at all. He just looked at me and laughed, and told me, You don't have to believe in God because he al-ready believes in you. I felt kind of sorry for the guy he spit on though. I don't know why. I think Mohammed was right about everybody wanting to make money off our unfortunate*

*black asses, but I don't think he deserved that. Before you
know it, I was just talking to the man. Telling him about
me, my life, why I was here. The man asked me if I thought
it was fair that I was punished for ending my family's suf-
fering. I surprised myself and told him I thought it was
fair—somebody should pay when a human life is taken, no
matter what the circumstances are. We talked for over an
hour, and he wanted permission to come talk to me again.
Why not? Maybe if somebody out there who's going through
the same shit hears my story, then maybe they won't make the
same mistake. Then I can say at least something came out of
this. I wouldn't wish this hell on my worst enemy.*

    Peace,
    Antonio

■

June 13, 1992

Hey Antonio. I hope you doing all right in there. I just
wanted to drop you a quick line to give you our new address in New York. No more 7th Ave, now it's all about
downtown, 110th Street. I like it. It's a lot quieter, not as
busy. I guess that's okay. You kind of grow out of all the
hustle and bustle after a while. I mean, it's far from everything, but there are a lot of negative influences out there
that I don't need to be around anyway. If I'm gonna go uptown, it's just to 145th Street to see Laneice or the Heights
to chill with Valencia at her spot. Valencia said she ain't

going back to Stony Brook. She said it's way too far and too boring for her. I could have told her Long Island wasn't exactly the spot, but I guess she didn't know. She said she really didn't like college that much anyway. It was too hard for her, I guess. She said she gonna do hair for a while in her aunt's shop on 114th and St. Nick. I guess that's cool, although I told her she should definitely try to finish college. But you know those Dominicans can do some hair, so I guess she'll be alright doing that. I probably won't see Tamika that much. She's staying out in Jersey for the summer cause she love it so much. The immersion program gave me a job this summer working in the office as a "youth advisor" they call me. Basically, that means I get to talk to the new kids about the program and do a lot of secretarial stuff around the office. It's really cool. My computer skills weren't on point when I went to college, and I paid for it big-time. I could barely type and didn't know anything about that Internet superhighway that's out now. Make sure you learn all that shit while you in the joint cause you gonna need it when you get out. Well, now that I'm working in this office, I'm learning a lot and I should be able to get a better work-study job when I get back. They're even gonna let me come on the Paris trip this summer and supervise the kids in the dorm we stayed in. So I have a lot of responsibility and that feels really good.

If you want me to, I can check in on your mother from time to time. Seems like Trevon has really been wilding out. I saw him the first night I got back. He was coming out of some bar on 8th Ave, eyes all red and smelling like liquor. He hugged me and all. He could barely stand and wanted to dance right there in the middle of the street. I led him back in the bar so he could sit down and get himself together. I asked him, "When the last time you been up there to see that crazy brother of yours?" and he said, "I couldn't even tell you. I done had a lot of shit to take care of, know what I'm saying." Then he just started talking to me all of a sudden, out of the blue. "I just been going through some shit, Natasha. I just been experiencing a lot on my mind." I said, "Talk to me. Tell me what you feeling, I got time." We ended up sitting there for a real long time. By the time we got to the end of our conversation, it had started drizzling a little bit and wasn't nobody on the street but gypsy cabs and hypes. He was talking about you a lot. "The man was my backbone. He was my backbone," he just kept on saying. I told him, "He can still be your backbone, Trevon. He ain't dead, he just locked up for a while. You gotta go see your brother and write to him and support him." He just said, "It ain't the same. It ain't the same as him being right there. Natasha, I lost my father and my brother at the same time. They was the men I needed. They was my backbone. I ain't got nobody to hold me up no more. I feel like one of them puppets on strings. My strings is cut and I can't do it alone." I tried to talk to him, but he just seemed so far gone it was no use. He kept saying that you were there—in jail—because of him. I kept telling him that what happened wasn't his fault, but I was tired and nothing was sinking in with him. I put him in a cab, gave the driver your address, and told the driver to take him home—nowhere else! No telling when the last time your mother seen him. Too bad it had to be like that. When he pulled off, he shouted out the window, "Tony didn't do it, Natasha." Why would he say some shit like that? I felt like somebody had slapped me and I couldn't believe he would play about some shit like that. I thought about what he said for a long time before I realized that he must just be too far gone and talking crazy. There's no way what he said is true, is there?

But I gotta go cause Mommy got *Boyz N the Hood* and that's my movie! Last week me and Laneice went and got the long box braids just like Brenda from 227. "Fly Girls"—that's what we been calling ourselves. You know Laneice happy that Black finally realized dissing her and Sharon was whack, so she been on cloud nine lately. I don't know why every time I sit down to write to you, I always say it's gonna be short. But it's never short. It end up being minutes and then hours that my hand is moving, writing letters to you, almost like *I'm* the puppet on the string and not even controlling myself. Just like when we first met and we sat on the phone all night, saying we were going to hang up and we never did. I guess I'm always going to feel special about you. I mean, you were my first. Daddy told me right before he died, "That first love is hard in every way. When it hit, it hit hard. And when it's over, it's the hardest to shake." Guess he was right.

Natasha

June 18, 1992

Happy birthday baby. Thought I forgot huh? You the only girl I ever bought shit for her birthday—remember that chain I paid forty dollars for on 149th and 3rd Avenue and I was all proud and shit when I gave it to you? Come to find out that motherfucker wasn't even real. Turned your neck green the next week and I wanted to kill that Arab who sold it to me. It took a little bit longer for the "A" medallion I bought you to go Irish on us too, but it did and I was so mad.

Anyway thanks for telling me about Trevon. I really don't know what to do about that situation though and it hurts me deep down in my heart. It sounds like you didn't believe him when he said he did it, which is good. Don't listen to anything he says. He's lost it. Can't nobody talk to him. I tried to tell my brother, Don't look at me and what I did and let that affect you and your life. Last time I saw him, I stared at him hard as I could and told him he better listen to me if it was the last thing he did in his life. I made him open his eyes and look at my face through that barrier. I asked him, Do you want to be in here? Do you want Ma coming and seeing you behind a wall? Do you want her crying every time she leave you? This ain't the life, this not the way, this not a joke, so get your shit together. Be a man. Be a better man than your brother. Take care of the family for me and Daddy. But it's clear he ain't heard a word I said. It's clear he gonna have to see for himself. It would break my heart to see him walking around a place like this, right next to me going through this bullshit. Now I know why my daddy smacked me in my mouth when I told him that when I grew up I wanted to be like him and work on the garbage trucks at night and get me a good city job. He smacked me in my mouth and told me not to ever say I wanted to be like him when I grew up. He told me it would break his heart to be at work and look over and see me working right next to him. He told me Boy you gonna be better than this, you gonna be better than me. Well, that's the same way I feel about Trevon. He gotta be twice the man I wished I could be.

I'm glad you took the time to write me. I knew you still loved me. I know we still got something. Tell the truth Natasha. Say I got out of here tomorrow. Say that by some crazy act of God, they let me out of this motherfucker. If I showed up at your door, would you still have me? Could I make love to you like I used to? No, better than I used to? It's been over two years since we been with each other baby. What I do to pass the time in here is lift, lift, lift. I passed 200, not bad for a lightweight. I'm aiming for 250 now. We got lifting contests and it ain't no amateur bullshit either. That shit is mad real and serious. When you lay down on that bench with all that weight against your chest, and it's up to you and you alone to push that shit up, and you gotta put all your love and all your hate and all your energy and passion into getting that weight up off your chest, you can feel like a god almost. That's why we do the shit and take it so serious. It make us feel like gods, if only for the few seconds it take us to lift some dumb weights a few times. The guards even be *cool with letting us have that protein shit to mix up in our juices. My arms is nice and big and round like melons. Nothing like they was before. My chest stick out like a soldier's. I'm all man now. Would you still have me? Could you handle it? Could you accept me now with all my faults and all my flaws and all my changes? Basically what I'm asking is, is there still hope for us?*

Answer me soon,

Antonio

■

June 27, 1992
Antonio,

I didn't mean for my letter to be some kind of tease. I know I'm the one who dumped on you, therefore I shouldn't act and talk like we're together when we're not. I didn't mean to lead you on, Antonio, and I'm sorry if I did. The truth is, I met a guy at school. His name is James and he's on the football team for our school. We do fun stuff together like go out to all the pizza places in Chicago and go to the movies and he even once took me to a Chicago Bulls basketball game. I'm surprised I met anybody cause it's only about forty black people in the college period, and only about ten black men. Well, I noticed him at the first Organization of Black Students meeting and he noticed me too. We got real tight. I mean, *real* tight, if you know what I mean. I think I was really upset about how my first relationship turned out, you know—us breaking up and everything. I was ready to try again and make sure it wasn't me that was the problem, that I could have a real relationship if I got the chance again. We ain't really together now cause he's from Chicago. We got a lot in common, me and him. He almost didn't want to hook up with me cause he was ashamed of where he lived. He live in these real tall apartment projects way on the other side of town. I mean, compared to New York, the pj's in Chicago ain't no joke. That shit is like a whole other country. No grass on the lawn, no playgrounds, the outside of the building look like a prison almost, with chain fences and high gates and barbed wire. But he said it was just something about me that let him know I would understand, and so we started spending time together and I like him a lot. I almost didn't want to come back to New York this summer, but I wanted to help out my moms and kick it with my friends cause this is my home and everybody here will always be special to me. He's supposed to come out here and visit me before we go back to school, cause he never been to New York. So I guess you could say it's serious.

I'm not telling you any of this to hurt you or anything. I'm just trying to let you know that you are special to me and you were my first, so you will always have that spot in my heart that nobody else can touch. I want to always be friends with you and know what's going on in your life. But that's all we can be. So I guess the an-

swer is no. If you showed up at my door, you couldn't
have me. I've moved on. And when you finally get out of
there, you will too. You can write me back if you still
want to be friends after what I just told you. That's just
the way it is.

Natasha

■

August 20, 1992
Antonio,

The more things change the more they stay the same. A
little girl is missing in our building—and this place was
supposed to be a step up. There's no escape, it seems. I got
woken up in the middle of the night last week. Cop cars
were everywhere outside at like three in the morning. I
thought I heard a baby crying, but I realized I was dream-
ing. What I really heard was this girl's mother screaming
and hollering about wanting her baby. Me and Mommy
and Roy had slipped on our clothes and went down there
to see what all the fuss was about. The woman was so out
of control that she basically started attacking people. Going from person to person in the crowd, grabbing them
and holding on tight, saying, "You seen my baby? You
know where she is?" She grabbed on me real fast, before I
could move. I mean, I saw her coming, but I couldn't
make my legs move. And when she grabbed me and
stared at me like she was in the worst pain you could

think of, I was frozen solid, stiff like old gum stuck to the bottom of my shoes. I just looked at her, stared at her really, and she stared at me back until she started crying. I whispered, "Ma'am, I don't know," before Roy grabbed her and took her back to the police. We walked back upstairs all quiet, my mother was complaining about "Lord things today," and Roy just said, "That's what we get for being nosy." We all just said good night and went to our rooms, but I didn't sleep.

Love,
Natasha

■

September 28, 1992,
Hey Antonio,

I'm writing you just to let you know what happened to the little girl in our building. I mean, just in case you were interested. I did mention it and it has been bothering me all summer. Even though I didn't know her, I would think about her all the time, on the train and stuff. But anyway they found her up on 113th and Madison, in this building that had been burned up. She was burned up too, but they could tell she had been raped and beaten before she was burned. Whoever took her had to have taken her right in front of our building cause she was only eleven and couldn't go far. And to think, that could have been me easily had we been living back there then. Eleven years old.

Burnt up in a building and dead. No future at all. Just eleven years old. I know you didn't know her, so you probably don't care. But I thought I should tell you just in case you had been thinking about it like I was.

Love,

N

PS. Her name was Jeri Lynne Jones.

February 1, 1993

Hey Antonio,

Guess you ain't gonna write me no more since I broke things off with you and I can't say I blame you for that. I feel real bad about it, but I miss your letters a lot, I guess. Life is good for me. I'm wearing my new FUBU For US By Us outfit and I just got an A on my calculus test! I'm cool in school and I got my own room this year. I am really, really thinking that I will be good at law. Thurgood Marshall just died. Remember we learned about him, the first black Supreme Court Justice. I think I can be the next, cause you KNOW it ain't gonna be another one of us for a long time. Just like they say it ain't gonna be another Dinkins for a long time. So I'm gonna work on being the next after Thurgood Marshall. That would make me the first black woman, so I would go in the history books.

Write me back if you feel like it,

Natasha

February 4, 1993

I know it's been a while since I wrote but back in June you pretty much summed up everything and told me what to do almost. Why do you keep writing me? What's in it for you? What, you feel sorry for me or something? It make you feel good to write me for your good deed of the day? You in college, you gotta man, you found somebody else, it's all butter with you. Can't you talk to your man now? What's his name, John or Joseph? Anyway, I don't care. I'm writing you back just to tell you that I ain't writing you no more. And don't write me anymore. You right, you moved on and I'm proud of you, kid. I can tell that just by reading your letters—you sound so sophisticated and shit now. But I don't want to be just friends. Hard time is hard enough without being reminded of what you missed out on. So you go ahead and do your thing. Have a nice life. Good luck with your relationship. I hope that shit works out. You might not believe me, but I really do hope that shit works out. I'm not trying to be sarcastic. If I ever meet him, it'll be all love. He'll have my respect. I'll just have to tell him, Man, you gotta good one and you better treat her right.

Love always,
Antonio

February 14, 1993
Antonio,

I was writing you because I thought we were friends, not because you're some kind of charity case to me. I told you I care about you and I will always care about you. We had something special, remember? I do. But you're right. I suppose it's not such a good idea to communicate with each other anymore. It's all good. Let's let bygones be bygones, the past be the past. Maybe I'll see you back uptown one day.

Goodbye,
Natasha
PS. ~~And maybe I still do love you.~~

PART FIVE

January 4, 1994
Antonio,

I just wanted to tell you that I'm so sorry to hear about your mother. The last time I saw her, she looked so healthy and full of life. You would have never thought anything was wrong. She had lost all that weight, and seemed like she was doing better than she ever had. You never told me she was diabetic. I guess she was so busy taking care of everybody else, she couldn't take care of herself. Mommy said her heart broke from all the pain she been through these last couple of years. Mommy told me one night Mrs. Lawrence just showed up at her door, late at night and out of the blue. Said she had on flip-flops and a house dress, but had her face made up like she was getting ready to go somewhere. She told my mother, "Denise, I just had to pull out my makeup bag and see if I could be fine again, like I used to be. I wanted to see if I could cover up all the ugly." She said something really disturbing: "I haven't done anything with my life—can't raise no kids, can't look halfway decent, couldn't keep a husband happy, couldn't keep my house in order. I wasted the one life God gave my soul." You know how my mother is, always listening to folks' problems and trying to make them feel better about it. She tried to tell her different, but it didn't work and they cried and got drunk all night, talking about the dreams they had when they were little girls, the dreams they had for their kids. I had never asked my mom what her dreams had been. Never ever had I even thought about her that way. She was always just "my mother," the one person in this whole wide world who would always be there. She told me that she had wanted to be in the FBI when she was little. She wanted to grow up and solve important crimes and go undercover. I never even thought of her as being interested in something like that, although she does like to do puzzles and play games like chess where you have to concentrate a lot. I asked her what Mrs. Lawrence had said her dreams were, and my mother told me she hadn't even said. Maybe your mother couldn't remember her dreams. Apparently, she went downhill fast after what happened to you. Things were looking up for a while, but I guess that was just all a front, a show. I wonder if anybody could have done something. Antonio, baby, all I could think about was you and how you must be feeling in there. I'm coming back to New York for the funeral. Mommy's giving me the money for the plane ticket. I'll see you then. Keep your head up, baby.

Love,
Natasha

January 7, 1994

Yeah, I'm bummed and down about Ma. My heart is real heavy right now, Natasha. Don't feel like writing much, but I wanted to say thank you for your concern. If they grant my furlough, I might see you at the funeral.

February 11, 1994

Antonio, I would say Happy Birthday, but I'm pretty sure you're not exactly thinking about that right now. I hope you like these books. I read them in a class I took. It was good to see you. It's been what—almost two years now since we were face to face? Although I guess you couldn't call you standing a hundred feet away with two police officers at your side as face to face, but you know what I mean. I was trying to catch your eye the whole time, from the moment I saw the police car pull up and you get out. I swear I thought it was going to rain, but your mother kept them clouds from breaking and ruining her home-going. She probably didn't want anyone to think she was crying for herself, so we wouldn't cry for her.

I hardly recognized you, you've gotten so buff. Laneice was like, "Damn, Antonio got cock diesel! You lucky he didn't look like that back in the day cause I might of had to hit that." I told her, "You wouldn't have had a chance."

But you still got them nice cheekbones, those big soft pretty lips like a girl's. Your eyes just look a little darker. When you did finally look at me, for that one brief moment, when you walked up to put that pink rose on your mother's casket, I felt a shot of electricity go up through me. Almost like God was speaking to me right at that second. If you asked me what He was saying, I couldn't even tell you. Maybe He was trying to tell me that I've been extremely blessed that my life turned out the way it has, that I was that one in a million who could make it out of the shit we had to go through, that I'm "better than blessed" as Grandma used to say all the time. Or maybe He wasn't speaking to me at all and it was just my imagination, or just me remembering how much I used to love you. I wish you could have stayed, I hate that they had to carry you away as soon as she was lowered in the grave and not a minute after. But I'll change the subject because I know you might not want to think about it.

I finally picked a major. Or "declared" my concentration as they say here. They have to make everything sound much more complicated than it is at this school. I'm going to major in "Law, Letters, and Society." Now, I know that's a little bit fancy sounding, but I really think I want to be a lawyer. There's no such thing as a prelaw major, but at least with this concentration I can study def philosophers and writers and geniuses and stuff to try to figure out how the world really works. I don't know if it's because of me knowing you or what, but I decided to take a class last quarter called "The American Justice System: Its Intellectual and Creative Debates." We got to read a lot of people. These books are from that class; I thought you might find them interesting. Remember that woman Angela Davis I told you about? We also read her. We read the *Autobiography of Malcolm X*, which you already know about. We read this play called *Short Eyes* by this Rican from New York named Miguel Pinero. We read this French guy named Michel Foucault, who wrote this book called *Discipline and Punish* that you should really read. I'm sure that Ms. Harris or Mohammed knows about it, and could find it for you. It was all about these medieval forms of punishment and how they compare to today. Do you know that if you would have been convicted of murder four hundred years ago, they could have sentenced you to "drawing and quartering"? That's a fancy way of saying that they tie each of your arms and legs up to a different horse, and then the horses run and pull in different directions—fighting against each other—until your ass is ripped apart. And before they do all that, they dig these sharp things called pincers into your legs and stick these hot irons in the wounds. I guess a dime upstate don't sound so bad compared to that, huh? Okay, I know that was a bad joke and I'm sorry. I just wish there was something—anything—I could do or say to make you see the positive side of things, the beauty and joy of the life you'll experience once you make it back to the outside. I guess I can't help but feel guilty that I'm here and you're there. I hope you do realize that there is light at the end of the tunnel. I hope you know you can survive anything.

Love,

Baby Girl

■

March 1, 1994

Sorry I took so long to write back but I couldn't think of nothing to say. I'll start with thanks for coming out to my mom's funeral. You really didn't have to do that and it really meant a lot to see you there. They wanted to deny me a furlough cause some motherfucker escaped a few weeks ago, so they got us on lock hard. I didn't write you back cause nothing could go in or come out of here for a long time. But I had a few people on my side to fight for me. It was good seeing everybody, even though nobody could touch me. I thought I would be embarrassed, showing up at my mother's funeral in handcuffs, but I really didn't give no fuck. I still felt like a free man cause I was around people who cared about me and love me and want me home. Being back at home for a minute and seeing people that I know love me made me wanna make it through this shit even more. I'm just sorry I had to see them under those circumstances. First time Black's shorty see her godfather, he's a prisoner. But that's alright. I'm gonna make it up to her when I get out. I'm gonna spoil her like she my own.

About my mother, I guess all I can say is that I have to

keep telling myself she didn't pass because of me. I know everything I put her through over the last few years was a strain. I made her tired. I wore her down. Trevon recognize his part in that too. He finally told me, I'm bout to do right big bro. I'm gonna do it for Ma, I'm going to be a man for Tyler. They probably gonna go stay with one of my uncles down South, which is a good thing. Get the hell out of Dodge for a while. See the world. Go places. Get out of your environment so you won't feel trapped by it. Wake up and hear some birds for a change. Walk on grass and not on concrete all the time. Open your front door in the morning and stand out on the porch in your boxers and breathe some fresh, wet morning air. That's the type of shit they need right now. That'll get they mind off things.

That means I won't have nobody to visit me for a while, which is alright. One thing I really been working on is getting the fuck out of here. Remember when that reporter came here and interviewed me for that documentary? Some big-time civil rights group saw the tape, and they came here talking about they want to take up my case. For free! So this group hooked me up with a new lawyer, this guy from the ACLU who been working on getting my plea overturned. He said that most of the time, that shit don't happen, but because I was so young there might be a chance. With my good behavior and my work and school record and Ms. Harris recommendation, I should get it. It's just a bunch of shit you gotta go through, a hearing and everything. I have to make a statement in front of a room full of people after my lawyers argue my case. He bought me a new *suit cause I've grown out of the only one I had, that one you and Ma bought me when I first got sent up. I'm confident I'll get it. I gotta believe in myself like you told me. Then I'm getting out of here and getting a good job. I'm gonna go get my brothers and take care of them and be a family again, just like Ma and Daddy would have wanted. I got my own cell now—I done graduated as they say. Benito finished his time. Mohammed's gone his lawyer got him approved for transfer to a work-release program.*

I feel like I've really grown up in here over the last few years. I thought a lot about what you wrote me about Trevon, about him saying he felt like a puppet on a string. That's all we really are in this life, although we try to fool ourselves into thinking that we're more. It's a higher power controlling the strings. We don't make the moves we want to make. And some of us, like me and you, get our strings cut when we least expect it. Some of us, like you, get new strings. Some like me just gotta make do and get through the best way we can. But this life ain't up to us. It's only so much we can do. You think if I had my way, I'd be 21-years-old and in here? You think I'd be without a mother or a father, missing my little brothers growing up? But that's the hand I was dealt. Some of us get better hands than others, and I'm glad you're playing your cards right. It sounds like you're gonna do really good in college and I know you'd be a good lawyer.

How's the hubby? Maybe it's none of my business, but you know I had to ask. Just wanna make sure he doing you

*right, that's all. Just wanted to make sure he treating you
like the woman you are.*

Thanks again for coming to my mother's services.

Love,

Antonio

*PS. I did look at you, for more than a brief moment. I tried
to catch your eyes too, but I guess we were just never able to
connect at the same time.*

▪

March 22, 1994

I'm going to keep this letter short because I'm actually
going through my finals study week now and I don't
have a lot of time. First, I don't mind you asking about
me and my boyfriend. There's nothing really to ask
about. He told me he wanted to do his "twenty-one-year-
old thing," whatever that means. I was like cool, cause
I'm handling my business and I'm not about to be crying
over nobody. Plus, he really hates the school anyway and
isn't doing too well. He's probably going to transfer. So
that's the end of that. As far as school, I'm taking the
maximum number of classes allowed each semester so I
can get the hell out of here a little early. I mean, what's
the point of spending money you don't have to?

It seems to me like you have things all figured out.
I'm happy for you and I hope you get parole so you can

get on with your life and start realizing your potential, which you haven't even begun to do yet. Right now, I'm taking this English class and learning about these American poets called transcendentalists. People like Walt Whitman, Ralph Waldo Emerson. We didn't learn shit about them back in high school. Well anyway, what these people believed is that the human soul and spirit had the power to mentally and spiritually rise above its circumstances, that the only limitations placed on human beings were placed by the human mind itself. I mean, these guys lived in the woods and shit and just concentrated on nature and spirituality and uplifting the mental. That's how they felt men (and women, too, I guess) should live their lives. I guess I been a transcendentalist before I even knew the word existed, cause I always felt deep down inside like I had the power to go beyond my environment. Maybe it's time you started feeling the same way.

With love,

Natasha

PS. The last time I saw your mother, I had just stopped by on a whim. She looked good, like I said, so I made sure I told her cause I wanted to keep her spirits up. She just kept saying, "Honey, I look good, but I got secrets. I got secrets tearing me up inside." Maybe she was hurting about something you didn't even know about. Maybe it wasn't you who broke her heart.

January 22, 1995

Natasha, I'm so nervous right now I don't know what to do. I know it's been a long time since we spoke, but I guess you was the only person I could think of to write and tell how I feel. I'm going to be up for parole soon, like within the next thirty days. This is it, baby. This is my chance to get out of here and get back on the outside. Ms. Harris said that she was gonna recommend me to get parole, and so was the supervisor of my work program. I already worked out in my head what I was gonna say. My lawyer had me write everything down and we been practicing almost every day, how I'm gonna say it word for word. But I don't need any practice. I could speak from my heart and tell it like it is. They gonna ask me do I feel sorry about what I did. I'm going to let them know that they have no idea how truly sorry I am for what I did and what I put everybody through. I'm going to tell them that five years up here wasn't my greatest punishment. My greatest punishment was looking in the mirror every day and living with what I did, knowing that I left my mother without a husband, even though he wasn't no good for her, but he was still her husband and I didn't have a right. I'm gonna let them know how much I hurt my family, and how I had to sit and stare at the ceilings and walls and think about that shit every day. I'm gonna tell them that if I could ever go back and change that night, I would have never come home, I would have never took that piece from Black's cousin, I would have never put a knife at my father's throat and said I hate you and let the blade sink into his skin. I would have never wrote out a plan to kill him in my note-book at school. I would have put my arms around him instead. I would have put my arms around him and said, Daddy I need you I love you I need you to love me too. I would have held him tight and my whole family tight together and I would have never let go until the fighting and cursing and arguing and money problems and shit stopped. Instead, I blew everything up. I ruined my brothers' lives, I killed my mother. I almost ruined yours, but you were wise enough to cut me loose. I'm going to beg them for another chance, another stab at my life. I don't want to let anyone down anymore. Keep your fingers crossed. Pray they let me out of here.

Love,

Antonio

PS. I'm going to try real hard to do that transcendentalist shit from now on. I'm going to go in there with my head up proud, I know I can be better than my environment. I'm going to set my mind free. I'm no longer going to feel like a damn puppet. I'm going to control the strings from now on.

Wish me luck,

Antonio

February 7, 1995

Hey Antonio,

I remembered your birthday is coming up so here's a card to say hi. I heard from Laneice that you got parole. Congratulations, baby, I always knew you could do it. I knew you wouldn't be behind bars for life. Remember when you went in and you thought it was all over? Well, now it really is all over. See, you made it through. I wish I could make the homecoming party Black's throwing for you, but unfortunately, I can't. I'm trying to graduate early, so I have to take finals for five classes in March. But have fun, enjoy yourself, and I'll see you around. I guess.

Love,

Natasha

July 11, 1995

I don't even know why I'm writing this cause you probably won't respond, but I was wondering if you wanted to get together and go out to dinner or something? I know you graduated from college and everything. Congratulations. I don't know if you're in New York or not, but if you are I really want to see you. Nothing serious, just get together for old times' sake. I'm staying with my uncle on 159th Street. You remember the apartment we used to come to every now and again when we wanted to be alone? He got me a job as a porter in these buildings on Convent. It's shitty, but I'm making enough ends to have some pocket change. It's off the books, so I don't have to worry about Uncle Sam scraping me. Soon as I got out, I went back to the block to check out whose there now, who been sent up, who's been a casualty of the streets. Same old same old. Black's laying low, got a side gig running for some Rican in the Bronx cause he got laid off from the MTA. He asked me if I wanted in. I told him I'd keep his game on the DL, but I ain't trying to have no part in it. The temptation to start slinging was there, but I'm trying to walk the straight and narrow. I just got out the joint so the last thing I want to do is deal with baseheads all day. For a while I didn't even leave my uncle's spot cause whenever I went outside, it felt like the streets was watching and calling my name. Right now, all I wanna do is be an example for my brothers. Trevon is at a community college down in VA now, and I can't let my fuckups affect him. When I get my own apartment, Tyler and Trevon are coming back to stay with me. So, shout out to a nigga when you get a chance. Let me know how you doing and if you want to get together sometime.

    Antonio

■

July 19, 1995

Hey Antonio. Mommy gave me your letter. I'm actually not in New York. I decided to take a summer internship at this law firm in Philadelphia. I'm going to the University of Pennsylvania to get my law degree. I come up to New York sometimes on the weekends, but not much because I'm working crazy hours at this place. Like fifteen a day and I even have to come in on weekends sometimes. I barely have time to sleep, let alone get on a train to New York. It's good to hear that you're doing all right for yourself though. I don't know, maybe the next time I'm in the city me, you, and Laneice and Black can all get together and do something, "for old times' sake" as you put it.

Natasha

October 16, 1995
Natasha,

I'm sorry to be writing on this poster, but I just gotta tell somebody about this and you the only person I know who actually will read a letter these days. But I'm at the Million Man March, you know, that big Farakkan thing everybody been talking about. I mean, I ain't no Muslim cause I always thought they was a little weird, but Mohammed had been calling me, telling me about this shit. Spread the information, he was saying when he called me cause we still politik from time to time. And me and Black was like, We ain't got shit else to do. Let's do some positive shit for a change. So we hopped one of them express trains to

D.C. at about midnight last night, just like that, on a whim, just so we could go to this shit and check it out. I'm running out of room so I'm gonna start writing on the back, but this shit is holy, Natasha. This shit is real it's love it's what I need what I been missing for so long. Brothers standing shoulder to shoulder like we ready to battle, like an army. It look like a flood of people so damn long and wide and far and deep and strong that nobody can break it down. I want all of us to leave here, Natasha, to walk arm in arm and tear this country down and rebuild it all over again, but this time with the odds in our favor. This time with the black man and his woman on top. And I want to apologize to you, Natasha, cause we talking about making peace with each other and our women. I want to apologize to everybody in my life for what I put them through. This day, this hour, this minute has made me a better man. There's not a man standing here who ain't crying. Including me.

In Solidarity,
Antonio
PS. Sorry I messed up your souvenir poster.

■

October 19, 1995

Antonio, thank you for my poster. I'm glad you got a chance to experience such an historic event; I can't imagine what it must have been like for you to be there. Getting your parole has done you some good, I see. Your writing even sounds different—hopeful and more alive. That's a good sign, Antonio. I'm happy for you, happier than you could ever know. I've hung your poster up, right above all my books, because yours is another story that the whole world needs to know.

Love,
Natasha

November 12, 1995
Dear Natasha,

I feel like Holden now, on an odyssey to find my place in the world. When a c.o. said Free Man walking on my way out, I almost didn't believe it. Inside, I lost my identity. I forgot the real me and the world outside, out of necessity really cause I wouldn't have made it through otherwise. Now, like Holden, I've gotten out and I have to search this city to find the real me. At first, I didn't want to leave my uncle's apt. I was used to being holed up in concrete, and something about the gates on the windows made me feel safe. One night I woke up and stared outside my window and the streetlights were shining on piles of garbage and their shadows looked like the guards that used to be a part of my life. And I thought, Oh, I'm back home. Then I threw up, right in the bed cause I couldn't make it to the toilet, because I knew it was sick to ever think about up-

state as home. When I got back from the March, all of that changed. I woke up early one morning and bought a pocket-ful of tokens, just so I could ride and ride and ride the trains all over New York City. The roar of the train, the energy of people fighting to get on and off, the rumble and the vibration shot through my body and made me remember there was blood flowing through my veins. I rode to the top of the Bronx, then back down to the edge of Brooklyn. I stood on the boardwalk and imagined I was an explorer staring at the end of the world. Then I turned my back to the water, and let the breeze hit me in the back. And I imagined the wind and the water were working together to push me forward, like the hand of God . . . further and further away from the end of the world and into a new be-ginning for me.

Love,
Antonio

December 21, 1995

Hey. Couldn't let a Christmas go by and not get you a card. Or send you a letter. I figured that just cause I'm not locked up no more, don't mean I can't write. Happy Holi-days. I hope it's a good one.

Love,
Antonio

June 18, 1996

Happy Birthday. Just wanted to check up on you, see how things was going. You almost a big-time lawyer now so I guess you ain't got time for a brother no more. I'm just kidding. Anyway, might as well tell you I got a shorty on the way. Before you break on me for getting some poor helpless girl pregnant, let me just tell you I'm happy about it and so is she. I hope it's a boy: Michael Antonio Lawrence III. I'm with this chick from around the way. Her name is Rhonda, and she treats me real good. She's a CNA now, but she trying to be a nurse. I don't know if it's gonna last. I met her a few months ago and felt like falling in love again and shit, having a female to depend on. We was both coming uptown on the A and she smiled at me, and we just struck up a conversation. It wasn't even about the yum-yum. I got out the joint and didn't even think about getting none. I just wanted to feel good about myself again. She's sweet and good and remind me a lot of you. I moved in with her, but I feel funny about this shit. I'm a man and I want my woman to be able to move in with me. But as I'm getting back on my feet, I have to realize manhood isn't just about what you got. She wants me to be there for her while she pregnant, and I'll do that for her if that's what she needs from me. So, we're gonna try to do this thing and see what happens. If the shit don't work out, I'll always have my kid, right?

Soon as I found out, I set out getting me a better job.

But I was walking around with nice shiny shoes on and khakis and shit, going to job fairs, filling out applications and having to leave half of it blank. Education, employment . . . I got all that in the joint. I can't let anybody know that. They had an open call or something like that for the City; I just walked out without filling out the application cause I couldn't leave it blank, but I damn sure couldn't fill it in. I just grabbed my coat and left without explaining shit. And forget about marking that box where they ask you if you ever been convicted of a crime. Nobody's going to see me, Antonio, and realize that I was just a kid who made a mistake. They're just going to see I've been convicted of a felony. I know, cause I had just two job interviews after filling out about forty applications—one at a hotel to be a doorman and another at this diner place in Midtown to wash dishes. And I saw the interviewer's eyes staring at me up over the application, knowing without even asking why I had left so much of the paper blank. Both of them just said, Thanks for coming in and they would call me if they need me. I been coming home every day asking my girl if anybody called, and of course nobody did. I came back from the march with a lot of hope. On the train ride back, me and Black even talked about how things was gonna be better, for both of us. Now, I'm not so sure. But no matter what, I will have my son. I'll school him about life way deeper than my pops schooled me.

Love,
Antonio

June 25, 1996

Natasha, have you ever been pissed off at God? I mean, keep it real, have you ever just wanted to reach up in the sky and pull him down off his high horse and ask him, Why me Why me Why me? Ma used to say, Man plans and God laughs. Well, he's been laughing at my black ass my whole life. I been looking for a gig since I got out, and I can't buy a break. And if I start doing some crooked shit cause that's looking to be bout the only thing I can get, then I gotta get caught and pay all over again. I've done my time, I've paid my debt, and all I'm asking for is a motherfuckin job so I can provide for my basic needs and get ready to bring a child into this world, and I can't get that shit? I want somebody to tell me why. I spent almost five years of my life behind bars, and I can live with that because somebody had to pay. But let me out and let me be free. Don't treat me like I'm still locked up. Don't judge me based upon the mistakes of my past. Would somebody tell God that?

July 3, 1996
Hey Antonio,

Congratulations on the baby, although I'll have to talk to you more about it later when I'm not so busy. I'm sorry I didn't get back to you sooner, but I can tell from your last letter that something needs to happen for you quick. Go see a guy named Eugene Spade at this place downtown called Second Chance. I don't know the address—you'll have to call information. I went to school with him in Chicago and now he's back in New York running his own nonprofit, an organization that helps people who've had a difficult start to find jobs. Tell him I sent you and lemme me know what happens.

    Gotta run,
    Natasha

July 8, 1996
Hey Natasha,

Were you in the city a few days ago? I thought I saw you, getting off the 3 at Penn Station. You got off the train on the downtown side and I was going back up. You had a short black jacket, your hair is much longer now, and some glasses (straight librarian style but still fly!)—but I still knew it was you. I jumped off my train and tried to run up the stairs to get to your side, but I don't know if you got back on or what. I waited at the top of the stairs to see if you would come up, but you never did.

Anyway, I went down to that place you told me about and Eugene is one cool brother. He got me a job the day after I went to see him. I'm working at this factory in Hunts

Point, marking boxes and loading up trucks. I'm only temporary now, but if I prove myself over a six-month period I can go permanent and get some benefits for my shorty. That'll be just in time for the baby. I been there early every day, and I took all the overtime I could get. I need this— big-time. That's all I'm focused on now. My seed and doing what I'm supposed to do. I wonder what would have happened if I would have never been sent upstate. I wonder if me and you would have a shorty together by now.

Peace,

Antonio

■

July 20, 1996
Hello Antonio,

Damn, baby! I did come up for a minute; I had an interview with a firm there even though I don't think I want to work in New York. That's such a coincidence that we were at the same place at the same time. Makes you wonder . . . But I can't believe you got a shorty on the way. Are we that old? I guess so. Well, you seem pretty happy about it and that's all that matters. I hope you and your child's mother can stay together, work things out, be the family you never had. Too many of our kids are growing up in broken homes and it means fewer of us are in law school and more of us are in jail. I'm doing okay. School is hard, but I like it. I want to do civil law, basically that means making sure that each and every citizen's rights are upheld. I would be lying if I said that what happened to you had nothing to do with my decision to go into that type of practice. But at least I'll be able to wake up every morning and say I believe in what I do. That's important. It's not as much money as I would like to be making, but I guess the money will come eventually and when God wants it to. It sounds like you're really happy. I'm glad you got on track. I really am. And to answer the question you posed at the end of your last letter, no—you and I WOULD NOT have a baby together right now. With work and school and internships and rent and everything else, I can't even THINK about that for a very long time. I can't believe you're having a kid. Didn't take you long to find somebody to "release" four, five years of sexual frustration with, I see. And you said you'd love me forever! I'm just kidding, and I know that time moves on and people and things change. I hope you have what you're looking for. Say hello to your brothers for me.

See you,

Natasha

PS. Sorry I wasn't able to return your call. How'd you get my number? I'm thinking Laneice, but she won't admit to it. Well, I probably won't be calling back anytime soon. I'm on a tight budget right now, and long distance isn't it. Plus I got a new love of my own who might get a little bit upset if I'm talking to an old flame in the wee hours of the morning. Maybe I'll hit you up when I get back to New York.

December 17, 1996

Hey Natasha. I never got that phone call from you, so I just figured you was too busy. It's all good. No love lost. But anyway, here it is. Michael Antonio Lawrence III. I knew it was gonna be a boy. Here's a picture of my son. He looks like his mother mostly, you can't see a lot of me in him. But that's okay. He's mine to take care of and I'm going to be responsible with mine. He's gonna have a better life than I did. If you in the city, come by and see him. Just don't say who you are cause I don't want his mama trippin.

    I can be proud to say I was there when he came into this world. I was in the delivery room and I saw everything and I even cut the cord. When he came out of his mother I wanted to be right there, up close, but I had to step back and let the docs do their jobs. There was thick blood and fluids everywhere, even on my hospital gown and my hands when I finished. I held him in my arms and listened to his beating heart before I passed him to Rhonda. I looked down at the blood on my body and hands and all I could think was the two most important events in my life covered me with blood. My son's birth day, and the day my father died. Only Natasha, my son will hear the truth. My son will never have any doubts about whether or not his father is a stonehearted killer. When he gets old enough to understand, I am going to tell him the story I never told you. I am going to tell him that I was fed up with the pain and the drama and the never-ending battles in my house. I am going to tell him about how I sat with Black and talked about getting that piece and planned on putting a bullet in my father's head the next time he pummeled my mother or me or my brothers. I'm going to tell him how I wrote it down too—premeditated as they say. And I'm going to tell him why I never got the chance. When I came home after the last time we saw each other, I heard the screaming before I even finished walking up the steps to my place. I opened the door and my father had my mother pinned down, her legs were trying to kick him off her from under the kitchen table. I had the gun in my jacket pocket, I could feel the cold slicing through the fabric like a knife. I heard Tyler crying, I heard Trevon screaming no. It felt like somebody was saying, Do it do it do it, in the same rhythm as my pulse. Then I stopped breathing and hearing and moving my own feet and all I could do was see. I saw Trevon walk real calm over to the kitchen drawer, where Ma kept her cooking stuff, and open it and pull out what musta been the biggest blade in there, and he stuck it in Daddy's back. Scared at first, so scared he let Daddy turn around. But then he knew it was life or death. I saw it in Daddy's eyes that he would kill my brother, but Trevon was out of control. He just kept jabbing and jabbing and jabbing until Daddy fell, and didn't get back up. I stood there and watched the whole thing. I stood there and let it happen. I was frozen, useless. I should have stopped Trevon. I should have prevented all of it from happening. But I didn't. So for that, I was guilty Natasha. It was my crime just as much as Trevon's. But Trevon is not as strong as I am; you seen that. He would have never made it with something like this over his head. He would have been out in the first round. We would have found him swinging from the ceiling after a few days in lockup. And I couldn't have that. So I took the rap. I told them what to say about how it went down, even though Ma begged me to let her do it. But I couldn't have her in there cause that's my mother and my brothers needed her. I didn't care about myself, cause I knew I was protecting my fam the way I didn't do before. And now I don't care who knows, cause I did the time and that's all the state cares about—that a nigga pays even if it's the wrong nigga. So they ain't gonna touch Trevon. So now I don't care who knows the truth. I wish I could have told you back then, Natasha, but I couldn't take the risk. That's too much to ask of anybody, so I didn't even ask it.

So I hope that makes a difference in how you feel about me, because I know no matter what you said you probably looked at me different. And I can't blame you. It's a horrible thing, but we ain't horrible people. Which is why it's important that my son knows why his father suffered, why he did what he did, and that sometimes in this life some things are bigger and more important than your one life could ever be.

Love,
Antonio

■

December 25, 1996
Antonio,

It's Christmas, and I've been driving all night. I've gotten engaged, and I was supposed to be spending Christmas Day meeting my fiancé's family. I've kidnapped his car. But when I opened your letter, hidden so well among the holiday mail, my mind lost control of my body. I started crying, and I couldn't articulate why. I just told the man that I think I love that I needed to go to New York. There was no question of what I had to do—I needed to see you. I needed to hear the truth come out of your mouth. I needed to hug you and kiss you and search your face to find some trace of innocence left—innocence you've sacrificed for so many others. The weather was hellish. Wet snow that wouldn't stick—the worst kind to drive in. I slid twice on the roads, and barely missed a deer on the Penna. But I kept driving. I had to.

I could hardly find the address on your letter because someone busted the building's stoop lights; so typical of the Harlem that I love and loathe at the same time. I found myself right around the corner from your old apartment. So many memories—good ones and bad— flooded me as I circled the familiar blocks trying to find parking. Over four hours of driving and I hadn't thought of one thing to say, but I buzzed your apartment anyway. After ten minutes of standing outside buzzing, an old woman let me in. She told me it was useless to buzz in this building because they never worked. I smiled and thanked her for rescuing me. She told me, "Merry Christmas," but I didn't even hear it until she had walked away. I walked up five flights of crumbling steps to get to your front door. The hallway was dark and there were no numbers, but I heard a baby crying and Pac coming from behind the door in the corner. I took a chance it was yours. It must have been minutes before I actually knocked.

I knew I had come to the right place when a woman opened the door holding a newborn wrapped in several blankets. I can see why you would deny your son's resemblance to yourself; he looks just like you and your father. You never mentioned Rhonda was so pretty, especially with the glow of new motherhood on her face. It was almost midnight, and it took me several seconds before I started to explain myself. "I'm an old friend of Antonio's," I blurted out when I realized she was about to go off on me in true uptown fashion. "He told me about the baby, and invited me to stop over. I'm in town for just one day and I wanted to drop off a gift," I lied. "Oh, Antonio's working overtime," she told me. "They get triple overtime on the holidays and we need it now." I smiled; I looked at the baby and understood.

She let me into the apartment even though I didn't ask. When I went to remove my coat, she told me not to bother. The boiler was broken again and there was no heat in the building. So we sat on the couch, together, shivering under a comforter, and then she asked a favor. "I'm glad you're here. Can you hold Mikey while I heat some water so I can wash him up? I don't like holding him close to fire and I don't want to leave him alone." For some reason, I didn't feel comfortable holding your son, but I did it anyway. He was so small, Antonio, so delicate and defenseless and helpless—everything you must have thought Trevon was. While she was gone, he started crying uncontrollably. She's spoiled him already, and he knew I wasn't his mother. She came back in time, and as she pulled out a breast in front of this stranger to feed your son, she asked me the question that started an all-night conversation: "So, how you know Tony?"

I told her a lot, mostly about us being friends and kids together, but I didn't tell her everything. There are things about us that I probably won't ever tell anybody. What I did tell her, I'm sure you'll hear about later. The whole time we were talking, I was looking around the apartment for signs of you—a picture, size 11 shoes resting at the door, a jacket thrown over a chair, a hairbrush, a scent. There was nothing. Everything was neatly put away, tucked in its place in your little domestic life. Finally, I asked to go to the bathroom, and I saw some cologne resting on the sink's ledge: Obsession, for men. I don't know why, but I put it in my purse—then thought twice and put it back. After two hours of talking and countless pictures and a few helpings of turkey and dressing, the baby was fussy and Rhonda was nodding off. She told me I didn't have to leave, that you should be home soon. I started to panic about seeing you again anyway, especially there in another woman's house. Antonio, Rhonda really loves you; I can see it all over her face. I thanked her and left, only to walk back after she shut the door. I wrote out a check for $100—the baby gift I was supposed to be there to drop off. I sat in my car for over an hour staring down the block, waiting for you to walk up the street, but then I was startled by two junkies who appeared out of nowhere to argue on my side of the car. I put the key in the ignition, started the engine, and headed to my mother's to "surprise" her even though I had told her she would be spending her first Christmas without me. I'll head back in the morning.

You don't have to bother to write back to thank me for the gift. You don't have to explain anything to me anymore. You don't have to believe that I never believed you did it, and even during the moments my mind started to wander slightly toward thinking that, I still loved the hell out of you anyway.

Merry Christmas,
Natasha

■

May 22, 1997
Hey Natasha,

You won't believe who I just ran into. Remember Mr. Cook? The English teacher who testified at my trial and came to visit me that one time. I saw him up on 125th Street, at the Mart. He said him and his wife had just bought a brownstone up by Mount Morris Park, and he was trying to decorate it. He was surprised to see me out, and I told him what had happened and how I had a bunch of people pulling for me. He said, God smiled down on you, Antonio, and I'm glad that you're going to get a chance to live your life before it's too late. He's not a teacher anymore. Now he works at this place downtown that helps people from other countries learn the language and get their GEDs and stuff. He told me they were always looking for tutors and program assistants and he remembered that I was "very intelligent." I laughed so hard, tears came out of my eyes when he said that. But he was like, No, Antonio, you were one of the brightest students I have ever had in my life. You just didn't apply yourself. Are you applying yourself now? No doubt, I told him. He said, Huh? I said, Yeah, I'm finally applying myself.

Peace out,
Antonio

■

August 28, 1997
Hey Natasha,

I saw an invitation to your wedding up at Laniece and Black's place. Sounds like it's gonna be hot. Way upstate? Honeymoon in Jamaica? Wow. I didn't even wanna know how much that cost, but Laniece said your man's people's was paying for the whole thing. Guess you hit the jackpot down there in law school. Found you somebody who could do something for you. Good work, kid, you deserve it.

Love,
Antonio

April 16, 1999

Hey Natasha. It's been a few years since we spoke to each other. I wanted to stop by that one Christmas after you came to my spot, which shocked the hell out of me for real, but then I figured you had already left and I was dog tired from working a double shift on Christmas anyway. I called your mother to try and get your number so I could call you, but she said that she had to check with you first. I don't know if she never told you, or if she told you and you don't want me calling you. I can understand if you don't. I mean, if you got a man, I don't want him assuming anything. I'll just let you know what's going on with me. I'm a supervisor at my job, which is sweet. More stability and more pay, so it's all good for now while I'm going to night school. I want to do some work with computers, make some real money. Michael going on three now. Here's a picture. When he was newborn I couldn't see myself in him and was wondering if he was mine at one point. But now he look just like his pops, right? What you think? Me and Rhonda ain't together no more, but that's okay. I had some issues with her dropping out of school and sitting on her ass at home all day. She claiming me and Mikey all she need, and I tried to tell her now wasn't the time to stop moving forward. I'm serious about making moves and elevating my status and she wasn't about that like I was, so I had to let her go. She's a good mother though, I gotta give her props for that. I guess her being gone got me thinking about old times right now, about how me and you was crazy in love like the world was gonna end if we couldn't be together. I don't think you can feel that type of shit more than once, after you have it once and get older and understand that nothing is forever and everything can end in the blink of an eye—life, love, security, you name it. I got your address from your mother. She act like she didn't want to give it to me seeing as though you married and all right now with your little house in Jersey, which I could understand. I just wanted to see how you were doing. Let you know how important you are to me. I know you think what we had was just some kiddy shit, some old puppy love. Maybe that's what it was to you. But for me, it was way more than that. Your letters got me through. Your love made me feel like a human being in my darkest hours and I swear I couldn't have survived that shit without you. I have each and every one of your letters, Natasha. All of them in a bag I won't let nobody open. I just want to see you again to thank you and let you know how much you helped a brother. That's all I want.

    Love,
    Antonio

■

May 17, 1999
Antonio,

First of all I just want to tell you you better not ever, ever, ever show up at my house unannounced again!

What if my husband would have been here? He would have kicked your black ass. Just cause he's an accountant, make no mistake he's from the hood too.

But I must admit that it was good to see you. When I opened the door, and you were standing there in front of me, I couldn't even catch my breath. Kind of the way you said you felt the first time you saw me. You are beautiful, Antonio. You really are. Even after everything you've been through, you're still the most handsome man I ever laid eyes on. Your embrace felt like being swallowed whole by something good and pure and kind and genuine. I lost myself in you for a moment—lost in your eyes that are still shining even after all you been through. Then I remembered where and who I was.

I wish you could have stayed longer. I wish we could have talked more. I wish I could have cried "I Love You" forever. I wish we could have taken a long drive on the turnpike and talked to each other forever like we used to. Part of me wishes we could have made love, slow and naughty like two grown folks who've finally realized what the good stuff is. But I know that wouldn't have been smart. That wouldn't have been wise. That wouldn't have been right. I love my husband, and I'm going to love the baby we have on the way, just like you love your son. And although I felt for you what I've felt for no man since, I can't walk away from all I've worked hard to build up. If you would have asked me ten or fifteen years ago, when my father died and I was living in that shelter, if I would have my own house and be able to make enough

money to help my mom pay for a house, I would have
laughed in your face. But I can. I do. I'm helping Drew
get through college. I'm going to put my kids through
college. I'm going to have that normal life I always
wanted, what I always dreamed about. I wish I could have
had that with you. If I could go back in time, I would
have that with you right now. But I have a good man. A
hardworking man and soon a child to think about. I wish
it could be so simple that I could have followed my heart
and followed you out the door, and we could go back to
Harlem to our tiny apartments where nothing mattered
in the world—nothing but the two of us, that is. But
that's not life. Shutting the door on the man you never
stopped loving, unfortunately, is.

I still have all your letters too, and that's how I'm going to have to remember you. Please don't come to my
house again. If you do, I might do something stupid like
run away with you.

Forever yours,
Natasha

■

May 21, 1999
Natasha,

*I hope you open this. I got your letter, and know that this is
the last one you'll ever get from me. I won't bother you ever
again. You finally made it clear. What we had was beau-*

tiful and necessary at the time, but it's over now. We aren't living in the past anymore. Now, it's all about the present—you got your life and I got mine. I got a son, an education to get, a job to maintain, a past to overcome. I apologize for showing up at your house without your consent, but I knew if I had asked to see you that you would have just blew me off.

Remember that time when we was walking home from school and we stopped by St. Nick Park to sit down for a minute and kiss? Remember that little white butterfly that came and sat on the back of the bench for a minute, then flew away when I tried to catch it for you? You told me that was the first butterfly you had ever seen in Harlem. It was the first one I had ever seen uptown too. I haven't seen one since.

Right now, it looks like the whole sky is filled with white butterflies. I'm standing at 158th and the George Washington Bridge, right at the walkway looking down at the water. I ripped all the letters you ever sent me up in little pieces, so small that anybody who finds a piece would barely be able to read the words. Little by little, I'm letting the wind carry the pieces away. They're flying and dancing and soaring like that butterfly we saw that day. I'm letting you go, Natasha. I'm finally letting go.

Love,

Antonio

1. Do you think Antonio and Natasha's love was real or puppy love? If he had never gone to jail, would they still be together?

2. How do you feel about what Antonio did after his father's murder? Given how things turned out for his family after his father's death, do you think he should have confessed? Should Trevon have paid for his role?

3. Why do you think the author chose to set the book in the early nineties? How would the book have been different if it had been set ten years later?

4. What is symbolic about the white butterfly?

5. What do you think about Benito and Mohammed? What kind of influence did they have on Antonio's transformation and vice versa?

6. How do you feel about prison conditions? Do you think that jail is an effective means of rehabilitation? Why or why not?

7. How do you think events in the early nineties, such as the release of Nelson Mandela, the Rodney King beatings, and the arrest of O. J. Simpson, affected the experiences of African American prisoners at the time?

8. If Natasha's father had lived, how do you think her life would be different?

9. If things had not unfolded as they did, do you think Antonio would have carried out his plans to kill his father anyway?

10. What do you think about Natasha's relationship with her mother? How do you feel about the way her mother handled conflicts in their home?

11. Do you think the death of Antonio's mother was his fault? How could she have handled the events of that fateful night, as well as the aftermath, differently?

12. Do you think Natasha was able to let go in the end as Antonio did? How do you see their lives playing out?

For more reading group suggestions visit
www.stmartins.com/smp/rgg.html

St. Martin's
Griffin